Dream Catchers

Dream Catchers

A
Journey Into Native American Spirituality

John James Stewart

PREMIUM PRESS AMERICA
NASHVILLE, TENNESSEE

Dream Catchers by John James Stewart
Copyright © 1998 John James Stewart
Updated Edition © 2009
Published by PREMIUM PRESS AMERICA

ISBN 978-1-887654-62-3
Library of Congress Catalog Card Number 99-70376

PREMIUM PRESS AMERICA *Gift/Souvenir* titles are available at special discounts for use as premiums, sales promotions, fund-raising, and education or for private labeling and licensing. For details contact The Publisher at P.O. Box 159015, Nashville, TN 37215 or call toll free 800.891.7323 or voice 615.256.8484 or fax 615.256.8624.

For additional *Gift/Souvenir* titles or more information go to
www.premiumpressamerica.com

Cover by John James Stewart
Layout by Booksetters / Booksetters@aol.com

Printed in the United States of America
7   8   9   10   / 10   09   08   07

These stories and legends have always belonged to the Native People of the Americas. And they always will.

Dedicated to:

The memory of Mary Davis, a Mushkeego Cree woman, from James Bay. She taught her grandson, Wapistan, the legends and he, in turn, shared that knowledge with me.

J.J.S.

Editor's Note: The writer and editors have attempted to present these legends in keeping with the spirit of the oral tradition under which they have been preserved and perpetuated through the generations. In doing so, some honorific titles and other proper nouns may vary slightly in capitalization, based on their usage and context.

Table of Contents

Foreword

by Lawrence Martin (Wapistan)
Mushkeego Grand Chief

I have always been a believer in fate, Creator's wish for something to happen. Many a time, I would watch events unfold around me, some which appeared to be negative but most positive. I would stand and wonder at the outcome, usually with a smile, always expecting another "fateful" action, solution and a meaning.

This is how I feel about my meeting with John Stewart. However, the first time I saw John, I thought Creator was being unkind to me, playing a joke, creating a most challenging opportunity for something ... but what?

When I delivered the sweetgrass to John, which his friend Mel Stewart from Sioux Lookout was giving to him, going to Nashville for the first time meant something else to me. I knew there would be contact with someone from the music industry and this would be a great opportunity to perhaps do something with my songs. In meeting John and explaining to him about the use of sweetgrass in ceremonies by the Cree, I forgot my excitement about being in Nashville. Instead, I felt a genuine interest in my own culture, in the ways of my People, and there was this bloke across the table from me asking all sorts of questions to which I was only too happy to respond. Nevertheless, when our conversation about three days later finally turned to music, he offered his help in exchange for my stories, but he strongly advised staying with the Native language and Native issues type of songs. During one of the evenings, he arranged with a tavern owner that I would sing a couple of my songs in Cree. I wasn't sure about that, after all, this was Nashville, and only cowboys and cowboy songs are cool in Nashville, right? Wrong! It felt so right to sing in Cree and in get those conservative-looking people to clap and chant to my tunes.

From then on, fate brought John up to Sioux Lookout where he and I talked about getting a greeting card business started utilizing the Native legends he had been unknowingly gathering for years; all we had to do was find Native artists to illustrate the legends. In working with John on the cards and on my music I have come to be a lot stronger in my own language and knowledge of my People; but I still find Creator's ways funny – He got me to go to Nashville to find myself and my roots? Strange, isn't it?

Lawrence went on to win a Juno Award, the most coveted music award in Canada, for his first album.

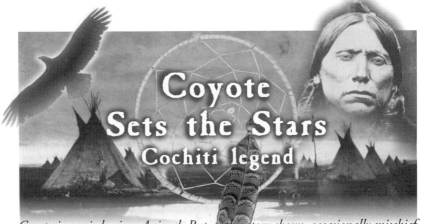

Coyote
Sets the Stars
Cochiti legend

Coyote is a mischevious Animal. But as this story shows, occasionally mischief can bring about beautiful things.

I n the beginning, only Animals, the Four-Legged, Birds, the Wing-Flappers and Fish People inhabited the surface of the Earth. When Creator made Humans, at first He placed them under the surface of Earth.

Earth Mother called a big meeting of the Four-Legged and Wing-Flappers and told them of Creator's intention to release the so-called Humans onto the surface of the planet to mingle with all the other Creatures that already lived there.

"What do we need them for?" whined Coyote. "We're doing just fine on our own. What are these Humans anyway? Are they good to eat?"

Earth Mother scolded, "Coyote, mind your manners. Creator tells me He has made these Humans in His own image, and they are to be respected by all you other creatures. The Humans have been given the ability to acquire more knowledge than anything He has made before. It will be interesting to see if they use it wisely."

Earth Mother brought the Leader of the Human People up to the surface of the planet. It was night and Moon shone down as brightly as Moon can shine. For the Leader of the Humans, this was the first time he had seen light and even the light from Moon almost blinded him. His eyes had never seen any kind of illumination before.

After a while, the Human Leader's eyes adjusted to the bright, unknown phenomenon. Mother Earth handed him a large pot full of bright, sparkling lights. "Do not look directly at these lights, Human. They will be much too bright for your weak eyes. Before the rest of the People can come to the surface, I want you to do something for Me. I want you to scatter these lights into the Heavens a few at a time. As you do this, you may give them names. These lights, when positioned, will be references to seasons and travel. They will become important aids to you."

The Man dipped his hand into the jar and scooped out a handful of bright, twinkling lights, never looking directly at them, still blinking and squinting through half-closed eyes at the extraordinary lights. He threw them into the air towards the Heavens. The Four-Leggeds and Wing-Flappers were hushed, intently watching as the bright, twinkling lights seemed to fly on their own. Higher and higher they went, eventually stopping and clustering together way up in the Heavens.

"So, what will you call them?" inquired Mother Earth.

"Coyote's sparkles!" interrupted Coyote.

"Hush, Coyote. I'm not talking to you. Take no notice, Human. What would you like to call them?" said Earth Mother, becoming more and more exasperated with Coyote's silly antics.

The Human Leader looked at the small, bright constellation for a moment, then said, "There are seven of them, so I will call them, Seven Lights."

"That is good, continue. Throw some more," said the smiling Earth Mother.

"Seven Lights. What a stupid name," snarled Coyote to himself. He, of course, was still snooping around, sniffing at the jar as the Human put his hand in to pull out more lights.

"Get out of here, Coyote. Shoo!" said Earth Mother who was becoming quite agitated with his foolishness. Of course, Coyote was, just as he is today, extremely nosy. He paced back and forth, sniffing the Human's legs, now and again snarling at him, then wagging his tail, not giving away his intentions and just generally being Coyote.

"I could do this, you know. We don't need this Human to do it," moaned Coyote to Earth Mother.

"Go away, Coyote. Mind your own business," She said in a very firm tone. Turning back to the Human Leader She ordered, "Throw some more."

The Human picked the largest of the sparkling lights from the jar. Coyote kept growling as though it was his job to guard the vessel. But, of course, he continued wagging his tail to and fro in mock friendship.

The Human threw the large shimmering light up into the Sky and, as before, it seemed to come alive after it left his hand, flying by itself up into the black, velvet-textured Sky. As the twinkling light settled just above the horizon, the Human turned to Earth Mother and said, "Before I name this light, please answer me this, is there a time when it will be lighter than it is now?"

"Of course there is! Daytime," said Coyote. "Don't you know anything?"

"Coyote," Earth Mother said angrily, Her stony stare quieting the boisterous canine but only for a very short spell. He went away, muttering to himself, "Stupid Humans, don't even know about day. Why Creator says we are supposed to respect them, I'll never know. Ha! Don't understand day! Ha."

"Don't take any notice of Coyote. He is always the same. But he is right. Day follows night and is much brighter than night. The first part of day is called morning. The last part, evening. Then, of course, we are back to night again. Dark, just like it is now."

"Then I will call this brightness, Morning Light," said the Human.

"That is a good name. It will be the brightest of all the lights or Stars as they are to be called. So, let's call this one, Morning Star. And the first ones you threw, Seven Stars."

The Human continued his task of positioning and naming Stars. He set and named quite a few, including a group called the Pot Rest Stars.

Meanwhile, Coyote was back at the jar sniffing around to see if these Star things had a scent of any kind. He put his paws up on the neck of the jar to see if he could look inside. Down it came with a crash, the clay pot breaking into many pieces and scattering the tiny lights all over. Coyote quickly tried to retrieve the twinkling lights but only managed to frighten them, making things worse. Off they flew, hither and yon, up into the Sky.

Which is why there are so many Stars in the Sky with no names. Nosy Coyote scattered them, scaring them away to the far reaches of the universe before they could be given their names by the Human Leader.

Chakabish
Snares the Sun
Cree legend

Why Mole looks the way she does.

Chakabish was now nine years old and he and his older sister had been sent by their parents to pick berries. With their basket full to the brim, they were on their way back to the village when they heard an eerie sound coming from the direction of their village.

They crept near to the encampment and from behind some bushes they saw the village was under attack by huge, fearsome Bears. The sounds they had heard were the screams of the terrified villagers being attacked by the Giant Bears. They were destroying everything in their path. The children saw their parents struck down, mauled and then eaten by the huge Bears. The Bears were killing everyone.

As you can imagine, the children were very frightened because they did not know what to do. So, they hid in the bush and watched the Bears kill and destroy everything. When nothing was left living or standing, the marauding Bears left. After seeing the last Bear leave, the two children entered the camp. It was torn to pieces. They looked around but could find nothing of their parents, save for a few strands of hair. Surveying all the death and destruction left them numb. Soon, the tears welled in their eyes and they sobbed freely, hugging each other for comfort. It was a terrible time.

A loud crack in the nearby bush brought them both back to their senses. They were terrified at the prospect of the Giant Bears returning and wondered what to do. Then, Chakabish's big sister said, "We should go from here because the Bears might come back. If they come back, they will kill us, too. We must quickly search through the broken teepee to salvage what we can so we may continue to live."

Upon digging around in the debris, they found some pots that were not broken, a bow and some arrows and some teepee bark and skins that were not damaged. They retrieved a snare that had belonged to their father. The snare was very special—it was made of sinew that had been blessed by a famous Medicine Man. It was said it came from a magical beast and possessed supernatural powers. And so, taking their meager belongings and, of course, the snare packed on their backs, they sadly started off with tears still in their eyes, leaving their one-time home behind. Foremost in their minds were thoughts of their mother and father, and it was with heavy hearts that they trekked along the rivers and by the lakes, over the hills and through the bush. Finally, they came to a spot that looked suitable for a campsite. The site was near a good stream of fast-running, cold, clear water. There were many medicinal and edible plants at hand. Both of them were very tired. There, they made camp. Chakabish cut poles for the teepee and his sister started a fire to warm them through the night ahead.

Chakabish was now the man of the family and went hunting and snaring every day for food. Each morning he would get up very early, leaving his sister in a sound sleep. He would return during the afternoon with Rabbit or Partridge and sometimes, larger quarry for them to eat.

One day Chakabish came back from hunting and excitedly told his sister about finding strange tracks leading into the nearby mountains.

"This animal must look like nothing I have ever seen before," he said. "Because of the kind of tracks it leaves, it is something that rolls. It doesn't seem to have any legs or feet and it scorches the earth as it passes over it. I must catch it. I will be known as a great hunter."

"No," his sister cautioned. "This legless thing may be a sacred being or a friend of the Giant Bears that killed our parents. You must not hunt this thing. It could bring disaster to us. Remember my words," she admonished.

Early the next morning, Chakabish left and went to find the peculiar tracks, not thinking or caring about what his sister had said. He found them leading into the mountains. He took his father's snare, the same one that had been blessed by the Medicine Man and placed it between the rocks where the tracks passed. He was determined to catch this strange thing, even though his sister had told him not to. He then went back to their encampment but said nothing of what he had done.

The next morning, before the light came, he got up and left the camp, going to where he had set his snare. As he got close to where the trap had been placed, he could hear a strange sizzling sound as though something was burning. Sure enough, he had caught the strange thing. It was a huge, red ball that angrily spat white hot plumes of fire into the inky Sky as it wriggled and struggled to get free but to no avail. It could not break the magical sinew of the snare.

Back at the camp, his sister got up at her usual time and went out to build a fire to cook something to eat. When she came out of the teepee, she was surprised to find that it was still quite dark, and there were no birds singing but she knew in her heart it was the same time that she always got up as she was well rested. "What could be wrong," she thought. "I always get up at this time of day. This is Summer. Sun should be peeking above the trees. It is always light when I get up."

Meanwhile, Chakabish realized he had snared Sun (Besim) but he didn't know what to do to free it. He tried to get near but it was too hot and he was driven back. All around him was dark. He wished he had listened to his sister. He worried everyone would blame him for making the Earth dark for the rest of time.

Some animals came by and told him Sun should be let loose or there would never be daylight again. "Chakabish, what have you done now? Let Sun go, right now!" they shouted.

"I did not know I was going to catch Sun when I set the snare. Now, it's too hot to get close enough to free it!"

"Chakabish," the animals said. "You must call Bear (Muskwa). Bear is very strong and will be able to get Besim free."

Chakabish responded by saying, "It was Bears that killed my parents. I do not wish to have anything to do with them."

"Those were Giant Bears. They are very bad. The Bear we talk about is Muskwa, Black Bear. Muskwa will try to help."

Muskwa was summoned and tried to free Sun but could not get close because of the great heat.

Another of the animals, Squirrel (Ah ji ji moosh), tried but he, too, was driven back by the intense heat, even burning his big, bushy tail.

So Weasel (Sing-goo-soo) stepped forward. She, too, tried and failed, burning her nose a little.

Then a very small Mole (Neh-paw-chin-knee-keh-soo) said she would try but the other Animals just laughed, saying, "If Muskwa can't do it, we are sure a little Mole can't. You are too small. You would burn up very quickly." The other Animals just ignored her.

"No," said Mole. "I can do it. We must get Sun free so there will be light in the Sky."

Fox (Makashoo) spoke up, "I'm a fast runner, and I can set Sun free." Makashoo set off, running at top speed toward Sun. But Sun again proved too hot for him. To this day, Fox's fur shows signs of the singeing it took from the intense heat.

All the animals were now very afraid there would never be light again. Again, Mole asked if she could try. Finally, they took a vote and it was decided to let her try. Neh-paw-chin-knee-keh-soo crept towards Sun, keeping herself very close to the ground. The animals watching could no longer see Neh-paw-chin-knee-keh-soo and they realized she had tunnelled under the ground a little to keep away from the scorching heat. Suddenly, without warning, the wondrous ball lifted from the ground like Eagle and it soared high into the Sky above the mountains. Everything below was bathed in its warmth and light.

Chakabish's sister was still back at their camp and was very happy to see the light return but she didn't understand what had happened, even though she thought her brother, who never listened to her, was probably responsible for whatever it was that had transpired.

"He's always up to something," she thought.

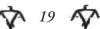

All the animals and Chakabish were very happy that Neh-paw-chin-knee-keh-soo, little Mole, had set Sun free. They all danced in celebration.

A short time later, along came Mole. She was in pretty bad shape. Her whiskers had been singed and some of her tail was burnt off. Her paws were scorched and were very pink and sore looking. Even today, all Moles still have brown teeth because of the intense heat that stained the brave, little Mole's sharp teeth when she cut Sun loose from Chakabish's snare. Her little nose has remained bright pink. The hair that used to cover it has never grown back.

Chakabish went back to his camp and told his sister what he had done. He also expressed his sorrow for what had happened and promised to listen to her more closely in the future.

After this great event, everybody, animals and the People, respected Mole. The little creature became an Animal Power to the People. It is said she gave her gift of being able to go anywhere and of bravery to the famous war Chief, Crazy Horse of the Oglala.

Butterflies
Papago legend

This legend teaches the lesson that giving a gift may be a great thing, but before you give it, think about who it may effect.

Elder Brother was out walking during the time that the rains come to the Land of the Papago. He was strolling along, just after a steady, two-day downpour. The rains had ceased, and Sun peeked out from behind the clouds. The mix of rain and Sun caused the flowers to bloom with truly vibrant colors and the trees and grass radiated their brightest greens. Of course, all the People and especially the children were happy to see the rain. The children were particularly pleased to see it because of the fun they have playing in the puddles and mud. The adults liked it because of its contribution toward a better life and, of course, the beauty it brings. It is a good time of the year.

Elder Brother came to a village and did what he loved to do. He sat and watched the children playing in the puddles or chasing and splashing each other, wrestling and just being children. "What a pity it is that Creator has given these creatures such a short Life Span here on Mother Earth. The flowers and trees, the birds and the animals, all eventually weaken and die. Such solemn reflections," He thought. "I will create something new to gladden my heart and make the children happy."

Elder Brother went off and collected some highly colored flower blossoms, some green grasses and some orange and yellow leaves which had fallen from the trees. He then collected beautiful bird songs, some blue from the Sky, white from the clouds, a little gold from the Sunlight and some silver from Moon. He put all these things into a bag then added just a pinch of finely ground corn meal and blessed the contents.

He returned to the village where the children were still playing. He gathered them around Him and to one little girl He handed the bag.

"Open it, Pretty One, there is something inside that should please you and all of your friends," He said, beaming with expectation. He stood back and watched as the little girl gently opened the bag in great anticipation. To the children's amazement, dancing flowers—Butterflies of all sizes and colors of Summer, Spring and Fallcame—out. As they flew about, the Butterflies all sang the beautiful songs of Birds. The wondrous, fluttering mass of color emerging from the bag delighted and exhilarated all the senses of the children.

Not long after this event, the birds went to Elder Brother and complained, "It is all very well to make such beautiful things. You have made these creatures with even brighter colors than we have and like us, you have given them the gift of flight. Can we at least have our songs just for us? After all, we had them first. The songs were given to us by you. Please let our songs set us apart from the Butterflies."

Elder Brother understood why the birds wanted to be different from the newly created Butterflies. And so, to this day, the Butterflies can fly as the birds do, but since that time, they have had no voice. Even so, their great beauty warms the hearts of all who see them.

Maheengun
Ojibwa legend

Sometimes, great pain and suffering is rewarded with a miracle.

Long before the white man came, some of the Anishinabe People (Ojibwa) had gone on a long hunting trip. They had been away for many Suns. At night, the hunters would dry and smoke the butchered meat of the Animals they had killed before moving on to new hunting areas. It was the Moon When the Leaves Fall and there had already been a snow. On the day I want to tell you about, they were paddling their canoes through a lake at Sunset. The long shadows cast by the fir, poplar and birch trees on the shoreline were filling the waters with black reflections of themselves, interspersed with bright red streaks of dazzling Sunlight. The smooth lake mirrored Sun's last, bright red rays. The brilliance of Sun's reflections and the glare from the pure white snow made it difficult to see the bank.

Squinting towards the shoreline, one of the hunters said, "It is time that we set camp." The others agreed and they turned their vessels towards the shore. He couldn't be sure but the hunter in the lead canoe thought he saw a wisp of smoke. He quickly signed the others to be on guard for the warlike Lakota (Sioux) were often in these Lands and had no love for the Anishinabe People. The feeling was mutual.

Pulling their canoes silently onto the shore downwind from the smoke, the hunters took their bows and fitted arrows in them. They, then, crept stealthily along to find out who had started the fire. To their delight, it turned out not to be an enemy but just a young boy. He appeared to be from a band other than theirs. He was definitely Anishinabe and no threat to grown men.

The hunters walked into the young boy's camp to introduce themselves. They meant the boy no harm. On reaching his fire, they were amazed to see the youngster appeared half starved. He was in rags and grunted his responses as he cowered under a filthy, tattered robe. The men set about making something to eat. The day's hunt had been successful and they had Deer and Moose meat. They also had many smaller game Birds and Animals.

"We will feed you. You will feast tonight," said one of the hunters, smiling at the still-terrified boy.

Shortly afterward, the boy, realizing the men meant him no harm, sat up from his blanket and began gnawing on a bone. The bone had no flesh on it, yet the boy crunched down his teeth upon it as if he were Wild Cat (Peshewh).

After a few moments, water was bubbling in the birch-bark kettle. Meat was cut and put into the water. More red-hot stones were dropped in to keep the water boiling. Some wild sage and onions were added to the broth. To the half-starved boy, the aroma from the soup cooking was overwhelming and he passed out.

One of the hunters noticed what had happened to the boy and picked up his limp, featherweight body and rocked him gently back and forth.

"I fear this boy is too close to death to save," he said sadly to his companions. The youngster was no more than skin and bones. After a few moments, the boy regained consciousness. The hunter asked, "What happened here, boy?"

In a very hoarse, soft voice the young lad replied while grunting like an animal between breaths, "I was hunting with my father. He was attacked and killed by Bear. It was a huge, ferocious monster, the likes of which I had never seen before. I managed to escape. After my father's death, I found the other hunters from our party and told them what had happened. One of the Warriors in the party who was also our Medicine Man had always coveted my mother and hated my father for marrying her. With my father dead, he saw an opportunity to have her for himself. He also saw his chance to get me out of his way at the same time. Under his guidance, the hunters held council to find out what had happened to my father. The outcome was that they said I should have been able to chase the Bear from my father and that it was my fault he had died in the wilderness. My punishment was to be banished from our Clan. I was left here to fend for myself or die. They left me with only a robe and bones to eat.

One of the hunters stood and said, "I know this boy tells the truth. The Medicine Man has already married the widowed mother. I was at their wedding some Round Moons ago. He is from a band of Anishinabe that lives to the South of where we live. I heard the Medicine Man is so powerful that all his People are frightened of him. That is why they went along with his scheme to leave the boy. It was a bad thing, to leave a small one like this to die."

The hunters tried to feed the boy some nourishing broth but he was so weak and had lost so much weight that he could not keep the liquid down. As soon as the hot soup hit his stomach, it was vomited back up. But he did fall to sleep, albeit a restless one.

Later that night, still cradled in a hunter's arms, the small, frail boy's breath started to come in short, hard bursts, almost like panting. He opened his eyes. They were a strange yellow. He spoke softly in a strange, growling manner and still grasped the bone he had been crunching on, "I have had a strange Dream," he said, "In it, just as they did in reality, my People left me here to die with only bones for me to eat. But in my dream, all was well, because the bones gave me nourishment. I was not in the form that I am now. I had become a Four-Legged. In the Dream, there were many of my kind. We were brave and cunning, much admired by the People and feared by other Animals whose flesh and bones we fed upon."

Then, the most startling thing happened. The boy disappeared from the hunter's arms. All the men were very frightened and looked around for the lad.

Shortly after the boy disappeared, from a nearby hilltop a loud howl was heard. In the bright Moonlight, a beautiful animal could be seen sitting in the snow, howling at the Moon. It was a creature none of the hunters had seen before.

Legend has it Great Spirit had made the poor, mistreated, half-starved boy into one of His greatest creations—Maheengun, the much-respected Wolf.

Shingebiss and the North Wind
Oji-Cree legend

This is a story about the rewards of diligent prayer and unwaivering faith.

There lived a very self-reliant bird, a Grebe named Shingebiss. He was a go-getter, a self-starter, not one to follow the feathered flock. There was certainly nothing sheep-like about this duck. Shingebiss was also a very devout duck. He prayed and sang songs of praise to Creator every day. For the most part he was a very happy waterfowl.

As I have told you, Shingebiss did not emulate others. And one of the things he didn't do that others of his kind did was go South for the Winter. He thought it was silly to have two Summers. This daring duck braved the very cold Winter in the frozen North. Shingebiss didn't mind it at all. In fact, he loved it, even though it was difficult to find food after the water on his lake had frozen over.

His faith was resolute. He would sing songs of praise to Creator as he looked for things to eat and he would always be given the gift of food.

One day Kewadin—North Wind—heard this cheerful duck singing and came down from the Heavens to have a closer look. There on the lake, waddling around was Shingebiss singing his songs of worship as he looked for food. "It's a grebe, I thought they had all gone South for the Winter. I will stop this silly bird's happiness," he said to himself. He then blew his cold breath across the lake, causing the water to freeze even deeper than it already was. Shingebiss kept singing, happily pulling up reeds from the ice and finding food in the water below.

Kewadin went blue in the face with anger and vowed to dampen the little duck's spirit. But that would have to wait until later; right now he had other things to do. There had been a snow ordered by Creator for a little further North, so he hurried off to carry out Creator's directive.

The next day, Kewadin came back and visited Shingebiss's lodge. He was disguised as another duck. He was greeted warmly by Shingebiss who invited him in to sit by his fire. While he wasn't looking, Kewadin would blow his cold breath on the fire trying to extinguish it. Each time he did this, Shingebiss would catch the fire just before it went out and stoke it up.

"I don't know what is wrong with my fire today," he said. "Usually I don't have this problem. My wood must be damp."

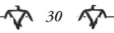

Kewadin was becoming very warm and beginning to sweat, "If I don't get away from this damned duck, I may dissolve," he thought.

The next morning Kewadin got up very early and blew all day across the lake that Shingebiss lived by, causing the ice to freeze to hitherto unknown depths. Still, the happy duck found food. He found it where, in the Summer, the water flowed from his lake into another by way of a small, usually fast-flowing river. The ice there was not as thick as it was in the rest of the lake. He was able to pull up some rushes and get at the food below the frozen surface.

North Wind was very angry because his power and authority were being thwarted by this very determined duck. Why couldn't he foil or freeze this absurd, purpose-bound bird? He had never had this problem before. Then something occurred to him. He wondered to himself if Creator was protecting Shingebiss. Kewadin went to Creator and asked.

"Of course I am," Creator answered. "He's a delightful duck, always extremely happy. His belief is unwavering, unshakable. He is my favorite duck. What's the matter Kewadin? Your authority being usurped?" Creator smiled.

And so it was that this devout duck's faith, with Creator's assistance, conquered the North Wind's hostilities.

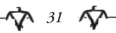

Keeper of the Medicine
Iroquois legend

Showing kindness to a stranger is a gift that is always returned.

I t was the time when the leaves fall. The wind had changed to the North and the lead-colored Sky drizzled a cold rain as the man approached the Iroquois village.

He was very old and walked with slow, hesitant steps. Even with the aid of his staff, walking was obviously an extremely painful experience. His robes were old and torn and he appeared to be very sick. He staggered to the first longhouse he came to and knocked upon its door. Above the door was the mark of the Wolf Clan. The door was opened by the Wolf Clan Mother.

"Please help me, My child," pleaded the Old Man. "I am cold and very hungry."

Taking one look at the bedraggled Old Man, she shouted angrily, "I have no time for beggars, be gone from here." With that said, she slammed the door, leaving the Old Man standing outside, soaked to the skin.

He shuffled sadly over the now muddy ground to the next longhouse. It belonged to the Turtle Clan. He knocked softly on the door. A young man opened it and again, the Old Man was rejected.

He then tried the Beaver Clan house and then, that of the Snipe. He had tried nearly all of the Iroquois Clans and every one of them had sent Him away, offering no help whatsoever.

He was stooped almost double in great pain when He knocked on the Bear Clan's Longhouse. When the door opened, there stood the Bear Clan Mother.

"Please, please help Me, My child," said the Old Man softly between body-racking coughs. The rain had now turned to a downpour, making the Old Man a sorry sight indeed.

"Come, in,' said the Clan Mother. He staggered forward and fell into her arms, His eyes closed. "Come, quick, help me with this Old One. He seems near to death. We must help Him." Her family gathered around the Old Man and two of her sons picked His limp body up and carried Him inside, sitting Him by the warm fire while the Clan Mother busied herself getting Him covered with some good, clean robes. She then took a cloth and bathed the Old Man's face. His eyes opened and he said, "Thank you, My daughter. You are very kind to help Me."

"Nonsense. Would You like something to eat? We have a nourishing soup on the hearth," she offered. "One as old as You should not be out in such weather."

"If it is not too much trouble, I would be very honored to eat with you," the Old Man said.

She ladled some hot broth into a bowl and fed the feeble figure before her, singing softly to Him as one would a child.

He seemed to get a little of His strength back and after she had finished feeding Him, He smiled warmly at her, then fell into a deep, coma-like sleep.

In the morning, He lay in His bedding, coughing. It was obvious to all that His health was worse. He was near death.

The kindly Clan Mother asked in a soft tone of voice, "Is there anything I can do for You, Grandfather? Anything at all?"

"Well, yes, there is something that will make Me well," He answered. "It is in the forest nearby. It is a plant. I will describe it to you and tell you where to find it and how to recognize it." He told her the information she would need and she set off to find it at once. She easily found the plant from the information the Old Man had provided and hurried back to her Longhouse.

The Old Man instructed the Clan Mother on how to administer the plant to Him. She followed His advice and was soon feeding Him a healing tea. As He swallowed the tea, He started to look better and better, younger and younger, until after swallowing the last drop, the once pathetic Old Man had become a handsome, Young Man. He said, "You have done well, My daughter. I have been instructed to stay among your Clan to teach you the healing powers of the Plant People. Their leaves, bark and roots have many virtues."

Creator had sent a Spirit to the Iroquois in the form of an Old Man to test the generosity of the Clans. For it was only to the compassionate that Creator would allow a great reward.

"But," the handsome, young Spirit, warned, "this gift must be shared among all the People, even those who shunned me as an Old Man. But from this day, the Bear Clan will forever be the Keepers of the Medicine."

Circle
Cree legend

This story beautifully captures the Native Americans respect for all life and the interdependence every Creature shares with one another.

The young boy followed closely, placing his small snowshoe-clad feet into the large indentations left by his Grandfather who was walking ahead of him.

"Look, Mooshoom (Grandfather), Waboose (Rabbit)," he said, pointing excitedly at Rabbit he had just seen crouched under a limb in the underbrush.

Grandfather said, "Shush, you will frighten it away. Today, you will become a hunter, Little One. Now do as I have instructed, pull your bow-string back slowly, allowing for the wind and the distance. But be careful."

The boy hurriedly let the arrow go and it sailed over Rabbit's head, embedding itself, quivering, in a large pine.

His Mooshoom smiled and said, "Well, my grandson. If the Cree ate trees, we would be very grateful to you for you have shot a very big one. Waboose is still there. Try again, only this time, take careful aim."

The boy did as he was ordered, pulling back slowly, taking careful aim and was successful. Rabbit jumped high into the air, mortally wounded. The boy's arrow had passed straight through the small animal.

Mooshoom beamed, "Go fetch Waboose, my boy. We will give thanks to Creator."

Mooshoom held the animal high and silently prayed for forgiveness for taking its life. He also prayed that its Spirit would become an animal again and then be allowed to return to the Land of the Cree. Mooshoom took his knife and cut one of the creature's front feet from its body, then tied the foot of the Rabbit into the boy's hair, saying to his grandson, "So the Spirit of Waboose and you will be one."

The very pleased youngster scrambled along in his Grandfather's footsteps, asking all kinds of questions. One of which was, "Why are there so many tips from the trees lying on the forest floor?"

To which Mooshoom answered, "Creator watches over us all. When it is very cold, He freezes the tops of the trees and causes the wind to break them."

"Why?" asked the little boy.

"For the little ones of the forest, Waboose and other small animals that would not be able to live without this gift."

"But Mooshoom, we have just killed Waboose. Will not Creator be angry?" inquired the confused youngster.

To which his Grandfather answered, "The killing was done so we may eat and it was done in a Sacred manner. Just as Waboose would not be able to live without the gift of the tree tops, we would not be able to live without the gift of Waboose. It is the Circle of Life and Death, Creator's plan."

In memory of Emile Nakogee, A Cree Elder,
who taught me this lesson.

How the Cree got Flowers.

Rainbow
Cree legend

The rain lashed ferociously at the teepee. The wind howled as it whipped across its open top. "It seems this storm will never let up," said the young mother-to-be between the pains as they came and went. She lay sweating, trying not to bear down, listening to her mother's advice and carefully following her instructions. Her mother guided her through her first birth. At last the wonderful moment arrived and, in the midst of the terrible, violent storm, a lovely Cree baby girl was born.

The husband of the young woman who had just delivered her first child was outside, weathering the raging storm. He had been shooed away from the birthing area for, unlike today, women did not want the added complications of silly comments or advice that males are apt to give at such important times. The husband was standing in the lee of the teepee, trying to keep out of the drenching rain. He was soaked to the skin. The downpour had lasted for many days but eventually, as He always does, Father Sun was trying to find a way out from behind the clouds.

He thought, "At least it seems to be brightening up. I hope my wife hurries with our baby as I would love to get into some dry clothes." It was then that a strange thing happened. The rain stopped and Sun peeked out from behind a charcoal-gray cloud. Immediately, a beautiful Rainbow appeared. But this Rainbow was different. Its colors were brighter and more glowing. One end of the Rainbow appeared to be right over his lodge. The other odd thing was, at the very moment the Rainbow materialized, he heard the first cry of his newborn. He rushed inside the teepee, anxious to see the baby but wondering what these weird phenomena meant.

The soggy but smiling husband took the tiny child from its mother's arms and held it close to him. "She is beautiful. She has your eyes," he said happily. He then continued, "There is a strange but beautiful, Rainbow hanging in the Sky, my wife. I have never seen anything like it before. It is so brilliant in color, it seems very close." He looked up and, sure enough, there, in the smoke-hole of their teepee, hung the end of the colorful Rainbow.

"Look, My Wife, it must be a sign from Creator. This child must be something special." His wife looked up and she, too, saw the strange, colorful sight. "We must call our little girl Rainbow, in Honor of this event," he continued as he hugged his newborn daughter.

As the years passed and the child grew, she would ask her parents and grandparents many questions about Rainbows. She seemed strangely preoccupied by them. The little girl's passion for Rainbows caused her to dash, at the first booming sound of Thunder, to the nearest hill to await the outcome of the storm, praying it would culminate in her heart's desire—a Rainbow.

"Who named you Rainbow? Why do you have so many colors? Why am I called Rainbow?" she would ask.

On one of these occasions, the little girl's Grandfather came to make sure she was safe after the storm had faded and heard her questioning the colorful spectrum. He smiled, then sat down with her and patiently explained some of her unanswered questions. He told her how Creator had earlier destroyed most life on Mother Earth.

He explained, "The Rainbow was first put into the Sky by Creator after the Great Flood. It was a sign to the People and animals who survived that there should never be need for a flood of that magnitude again. It is called Rainbow because it is shaped like a bow and arrives after the rain—rain-bow. You, Rainbow, were born just after a very violent storm. It was a storm so ferocious that we began to wonder if Creator was going to destroy us again. But as the rain and wind ebbed, a beautiful Rainbow appeared and you were named after it. Why the colors are such, I do not know. I have never seen them anywhere else on Earth."

The little girl seemed content with her Grandfather's answers and, after the Rainbow faded, she returned with him to her lodge, happily sloshing along by his side over the rain-soaked ground.

"I always feel happy when the Rainbow visits. It's like I'm part of it. It seems to want to see me," she confided in her Grandfather.

Not long after her Grandfather had explained all this to her, Rainbow was playing near her village when a loud crack of Thunder reverberated overhead. Off she dashed to the nearest peak and sat down to await the storm's outcome. The rains lashed the prairie below. The dark clouds seemed to roll while being savagely pushed by the vicious winds. It became very dark and the wind dropped to nothing. The little girl, for the first time, became afraid. Suddenly, the air was filled with a strange sound. Overhead, she heard giant wings flapping. She turned her rain-splattered face towards the frightening sound. Huge talons grasped her small body and jerked her free from her position. Up into the Sky flew the creature through the now-silent, black thunderclouds, its wings beating powerfully. The Thunderbird flew towards the Land of the Rainbow.

When the Thunderbird arrived at its destination in the Sky, it lightly placed the little girl down among soft, billowing, colored clouds. Many other Thunderbirds gathered around her. She was very frightened. One extremely large Thunderbird stepped forward. She knew, instinctively that it must be the Leader.

"Do not fear, Rainbow." He paused and smiled. "By the confused look on your face, you are wondering how we know who you are? It is simple, you are one of us. You belong here in the Land of the Rainbow." The Thunderbird laughed. "Of course I don't mean you are a Thunderbird, but your thoughts about the Rainbow were correct and you are part of it. It gave you life. You will be very happy here, all your questions will be answered in time."

Just as the Thunderbird Leader had said, the little girl did settle down and quickly became staunch friends with all the Thunderbirds. She was very happy in her new Land.

One day she was sitting on the edge of the Rainbow looking down at Earth, thinking about her family, but mostly about her beloved Grandfather. She did not notice the Thunderbird Leader approach and was a little startled when he spoke, "Are you not happy here, My Child?"

"Oh, yes, of course I am," she said, gathering her composure. "But I do miss my family, especially my Grandfather. I wish I could do something to tell them that I am all right, that I am happy."

"Well, that's what you shall do. Take a handful of Rainbow and, just before Father Sun goes down, let it go. Let it fall toward Earth. I will do the rest." That evening the little girl did as she was told. She took a handful of colorful Rainbow dust and let it fall, sifting through her fingers. The dust floated gently to Earth, landing near the lodge of the little girl's family.

The next morning was warm and Sunny. The little girl's Grandfather was out walking. As always, he was looking for clues that could shed some light on his granddaughter's mysterious disappearance. He walked along the usual route she took when the storms came to the Cree Lands. As he turned at a bend in the trail, there, to his amazement, lay a nest of strange vegetation, plants he had never seen the like of before—yellow, red, violet, orange, all the colors of the Rainbow. He knew, immediately, that it was a sign that all was well with his little friend, his beautiful granddaughter. He hurried off to give his family the wonderful news.

And so, the little girl, Rainbow, is easily remembered by the Cree People for she gave them a beautiful gift, something to brighten their lives—flowers.

The Little Girl who Loved the Star

Chipewyan legend

This tale shows that the love of a friend is a treasure beyond words. It also describes St. Elmo's Fire, a natural, visible electric discharge emanating from a pointed object such as the mast of a ship or the wing of an airplane during an electrical storm.

The Stars were trying to organize themselves in a more politically inclined, governmental way and there had been a terrible quarrel among them about who should be in charge. The larger Stars, of course, thought it should be one of them; the smaller Stars, who were much more numerous, said it should be the brightest, cleverest Star that commanded, not necessarily the biggest.

There was one tiny, very bright Star that the larger Stars were jealous of, as they knew that one night it could be chosen to lead all the celestial bodies. It was very popular among all the small Stars, the nebula and asteroids. In fact, it was so revered among them that the larger Stars formed an alliance to counter its attraction. This alliance was more like a mob, a gang. This constellation of large Stars conspired against the small, bright Star. Through lies and manipulation, the big Stars managed to convince the smaller ones that the tiny, bright Star was wicked, corrupt and full of evil. So successful was their campaign that they forced the little Star to leave the Heavens under threat of destruction from all the others. And so, the larger, bullying gang Stars had won the day and the rejected one descended to Earth.

Once on Earth the little Star tried to make the best of its new life but it was very lonely. It felt abandoned. It found the Land of the Chipewyan and moved about among them, looking for someone to play with. Sometimes, it tried to play and make friends with the Native children by landing on their heads. But the children, not being used to this kind of thing, would run to their mothers. They were very afraid of the little Star. It, on the other hand, was frightened of adult People, viewing them as unfriendly giants.

Among the Chipewyan lived a small girl who, like the Star, was very forlorn. Her grandparents were both deceased and her mother had recently passed away. She had no brothers or sisters and her father was always busy hunting. She was nearly always taken along with him as she had no one else to look after her. Of course, in the remote hunting camps there were seldom other children to play with. She would be left alone time after time; she was desperately lonely.

One evening just after Sunset, the Star came across the small hunting camp and saw the little girl as she stood outside her father's Lodge, waiting for him and the other hunters to return. When the Star first saw the little girl, she looked so sorrowful that it momentarily forgot its own sadness and was overcome with the need to cheer up the youngster.

"Creator, please don't let her be frightened of me, let her accept me for what I am," the Star silently prayed. "I am desperately in need of a friend and this child appears to have the same need." It sidled up to the little girl and landed on her head. The Star's wish was granted. The child did not cry or run away. Instead, she reached up and picked the bright, shining light off her head and studied it closely, smiling, something she had not done for a very long time.

"What a beautiful, twinkling light you have," said the little girl. "It shimmers like snow crystals in the Sunlight. What are you? Will you be my friend?" The words gushed and bubbled from her like a fast-flowing stream. "I am very lonely as everyone that I ever loved is dead, except for my father, and he is always away, busy hunting. I have no one to play with. Will you play with me?"

Of course, the little Star couldn't answer her questions as it had no voice that a Human could understand. But understand the child, it certainly did. It was beside itself with happiness. From that day on it had a true friend. It followed the little girl wherever she went. They would play for hours on end, chasing each other around, hiding from one another, although the Star was not very good at hiding as its glow would always give away its hiding place. The Star didn't care. It was happy at last and so was the little girl. She loved the tiny Star with all her heart. At night, if the little girl woke and opened her eyes, there, right above her head, was her little, twinkling friend looking just as content as a

Star could be. The loneliness that had bonded the pair together was now a thing of the past for both of them. True happiness reigned.

Soon, the child found herself sharing the Star with her father, for it had strange powers over the game animals. From then on, the little girl's father was blessed with great hunting skills as the animals would give themselves freely to him whenever the little Star was near. So, even the father now had more time to spend with his young daughter. He thought the Star was a gift to his family from Great Spirit.

One morning father asked his daughter to go out and pick berries. "Leave the Star with me," her father said. "I will need its help in my hunting today. With the Star along, it will not take long to find meat. We will all play some games when I get back this afternoon when we will have time together to enjoy each other's company."

Off went the little girl with her basket to the nearby lake where she knew there would be lots of berries. She was sad she couldn't take her friend with her, but understood her father needed the Star's skills in finding game. She went out into the woods toward the lake, all the while looking forward to returning to the village and playing with her father and her celestial friend.

She soon reached the lake and began picking berries of all sorts where they grew in abundance in the soggy, bog-like ground along the shore. Some of the Cranberry bushes even grew out into the water, so she waded out to get them, knowing they were her father's favorite. All the time the little girl was picking berries, she was thinking of the games that she and the Star would play when she got back to the village. She was very happy in her revery.

Suddenly, not watching where she was walking, she slipped into a deep hole. Gooey mud started to swallow her, pulling her down into its depths. As she struggled, she went deeper and deeper. Soon, the water covered her head and the little girl, who loved the Star, was drowned.

Father Sun had just reached the center of the Sky when the girl's father returned to his camp carrying a Deer the little Star had led him to. He was looking forward to the quality time that the little Star now afforded his family. He looked around and shouted for his child to come and see. Of course, she didn't come. He asked his neighbors and friends if they had seen his daughter. "She should have been back by now," he said. The worried father quickly formed a search party when he realized his daughter was missing. They looked for the little girl for days and days. The tiny Star was always out in front of the search party, inspecting every nook and cranny. Of course, the little girl was never found.

After the loss of its friend, the Star remained with the little girl's father for some time, hovering just above the village where the little girl had lived, hoping for a miracle that would return its beloved friend. But from the day of the terrible accident, the glow from the Star never shone as brightly as it had when its best friend was alive. Soon, the Star set off on a never-ending quest, searching for its friend. In the Winter, hunters often see the lonely, heartbroken Star as it moves close to the ground, still looking for the little girl it adored.

Cheecheeshkishee
Ojibwa/Cree legend

As this story demonstrates, vanity and dishonesty have always been the source of trouble, regardless of what Tribe you are from.

Before the Human People came, the birds had a Leader called Washeshkut (Belly Showing). He was very conceited and ruled in a high-handed manner. As you can imagine, he was not well-liked. Washeshkut had a beautiful daughter but much like her father, she, too, was exceedingly arrogant. The other birds would come and ask for her wing in marriage but she always turned them down.

"I am far too good for you," she would say. "Just look at yourself. You are so unattractive whereas I am stunning. I could never let myself even be seen with the likes of you, you ugly Buzzard." Obviously, these cutting comments upset a lot of the Bird Tribe and certainly disturbed the Buzzards.

Even her conceited father was becoming worried she might never wed. "Would you marry anyone? Is there any bird that you like at all?" he asked anxiously.

"Well, Maang (Loon) is the most handsome of all the birds. But he is already married and anyway, he has never asked me," she said.

To which her father said, "I wonder what he would do if his wife met with an accident? Suppose she was killed. He would then have to look elsewhere for a wife," he said and they both laughed at her father's deviousness.

"Well, my beautiful one, let's have some fun with our People. We'll have a competition that no one can win, save, maybe for Maang," said her father in a mysterious voice.

"What will the competition be?" she asked.

"It will be a guessing game. I will tell the People whoever can guess my pet name for you, Gageninagage (She-Who-Has-the-Gift), a name I have never uttered in anyone's presence but yours, can marry you."

"I don't wish to marry any of these foul-looking birds," she said obstinately, then, pouting, added "I want Maang."

"Not so fast, daughter. I will fix this contest so handsome Maang wins. He will take you as his wife," answered her father.

"He is already married. How can you fix it?" she asked, still sulking.

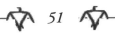 51

"You are so beautiful that I think Maang will take two wives. I am sure that when you become his wife, he will soon tire of his other one and give her back to her parents." And so, the deceitful pair plotted into the night. The next morning the contest was announced to the Tribe. All the handsome young birds donned their thinking caps.

Cheecheeshkishee (Sandpiper) lived near the Chief and his daughter. He was a funny little bird, laughed at by most, always rushing around, following the waves as they washed in and out on the shore where he pecked at the microscopic bits of food that drifted in. Cheecheeshkishee never ever flew unless it was really necessary. Even then, he never flew very high. The other birds thought he was not right in the head. They would laugh and tease him over his silly antics. Sandpiper was thought to be a very unconventional bird.

Many birds wondered why Sandpiper ran so fast all the time. The answer was simple. The one thing Cheecheeshkishee truly hated above all things was getting his feet wet. So, he darted in and out, just in front of the rolling waves as they surged onto the beach. He moved as fast as his little, dry feet would carry him, never allowing the waves to break over them.

A short time after the Chief made his announcement about the contest, Cheecheeshkishee was, as always, looking for food, rushing in and out of the waves as they broke on the shore. On one of his mad dashes back toward the beach, just inches ahead of the oncoming water, Cheecheeshkishee noticed Spider nonchalantly wandering along the beach. He dashed toward it with lunch on his mind. He was just about to devour the hairy-legged creature, when Spider, realizing he was trapped, got down on eight-bended knees and begged to be spared, pleading for his life.

"If I spare you," said Cheecheeshkishee, considering his options, "you must do something for me."

"I will do anything you ask, Oh mighty one. Please don't eat me," gasped the terrified Spider.

"I will make a deal with you. If you do this for me, I won't eat you. I want you to literally hang around in the Chief's lodge, hang from the roof on one of your silky threads and eavesdrop. I want you to find out the pet name the Chief has for his conceited daughter. There is to be a contest ...." Cheecheeshkishee laid out his strategy to Spider for winning the competition, then asked, "Can you do that, you fuzzy little fellow?"

"Of course I can! It's a deal," said the thankful Spider, speeding silently sideways, just as fast as his eight, hairy legs would carry him to the Lodge of Belly Showing, all the while thanking Creator and Cheecheeshkishee for sparing his life.

Spider soon made a web in the top of Belly Showing's Lodge and set up his listening post. That night Spider stayed up very late, listening and watching intently but the daughter's pet name was never mentioned. Eventually, Spider could keep none of his many eyes open, he was so tired.

Yawning deeply, he spun himself a little hammock, jumped in and was soon sound asleep, rocking gently in his gossamer bed.

The next morning the Chief and his daughter were sitting having some food with Spider still snooping from above. Chief said, "None of my silly Bird Tribe will ever guess that my pet name for you is Gageninagage. Maang will win. All I have to do is make him guess your name. Whatever he says, he will win. As nobody knows your pet name, I can tell them anything!"

"That's it!" thought Spider. With the information gathered, the spying Spider spun a thin strand of silk, then descended quickly to the Lodge floor below where he scuttled off to tell Cheecheeshkishee the pet name and how dishonest the Chief intended to be.

"So, her name is Gageninagage! Good, now I will have some fun," said Sandpiper.

"You're not really going to marry that conceited bird are you?" asked Spider.

"That remains to be seen. I hope not. We'll have to see. Now, get out of here before I change my mind and munch a Spider for lunch."

On the day of the contest, many of the most handsome birds from the Tribe were outside the Chief's Lodge. All the birds thought very highly of themselves. Wood Duck, Eagle, Raven and Snow Goose stood about, proudly preening themselves, awaiting their opportunity to guess the beautiful girl's name.

The Chief came out of his lodge, followed by his exquisite-looking daughter. "Let the contest begin," he said.

Raven stepped up, "I think her name is Pretty One."

"No, that's not it," said the Chief. "Whose next?"

"How about Pretty Feather?" said Eagle.

"No, that's not it either," said the now-smiling Chief.

"I know," said Sandpiper.

"How about you, Blue Jay?" asked the Chief, ignoring Cheecheeshkishee.

"Is it Fair Maid?" asked Blue Jay.

"No."

"I would like a turn," interrupted Cheecheeshkishee.

Again, the Chief completely ignored him. Some of the other birds said rude things to Sandpiper, including Eagle, who said, "Why don't you run on home, Cheecheeshkishee. You will never guess her name, you silly bird."

All the Birds took turns trying to guess the beautiful girl's name, all save Maang who seemed disinterested and Cheecheeshkishee, who wasn't given the opportunity.

Maang was standing on the perimeter of the gathering, impartially watching the proceedings.

"How about you, Maang? Why don't you guess her name?" shouted the Chief.

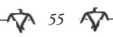

"I have a wife, I do not need another," said Maang.

"Well, maybe it's time you took another. A great person like yourself should be able to take care of at least two wives. They could keep each other company while you are away hunting," laughed the Chief.

"I do not need another wife, but if I were to guess, I would say her name would be One-Who-Thinks-Highly-Of-Herself," said Maang, smiling to himself over his veiled insult.

The Chief, without even thinking over what Loon had said, replied, "Well, Maang, you are very close. So, as no one has gottten as close as you, I declare you the winner."

"Her name is actually Gageninagage," interrupted Cheecheeshkishee, in a very matter-of-fact manner.

A hush came over the crowd. Everyone turned toward Cheecheeshkishee. The name he had uttered was obviously the correct one, judging from the astonished looks on the faces of the Chief and his daughter.

"How did you find out my name, you creepy little bird? I will never marry you," screamed the beautiful, disdainful daughter as she rushed off and went into the Lodge. "I want to marry Maang," she sobbed.

"You will do as you are told," her father shouted after her. Then, addressing Cheecheeshkishee, he said, "So, you have won my beautiful daughter. Who would have thought a stupid bird such as yourself would end up winning such a wonderful prize. But, I will honor my word."

Sandpiper again interrupted "How dare you call me stupid! Just because I'm different from the other birds does not make me stupid. Think about this, Oh Wise Chief, I was the only Bird who figured out your arrogant daughter's name. Rest assured, I do not wish to marry her. She is far too conceited for me. But one thing I do ask, in fact, demand is that from now on I will be treated as the other birds are treated. I am not and never was inferior to anyone. Just because I don't like getting my feet wet does not make me peculiar. From here on in, I want to be treated with respect. If you do not promise that, I will marry your daughter, right now, just for spite."

It was obvious to the Chief that Sandpiper meant every word he said. The Chief, not wanting to deal with his distraught daughter, said, "Well, I suppose that will be all right. I've always thought you were a bright bird. I really respect you." Obviously not meaning a word he had said to Sandpiper, the Chief turned to Maang and continued, "Now, Maang, what about my daughter?"

Maang spoke up, addressing the Chief and Sandpiper, "Cheecheeshkishee, I must admit, I never thought you would turn out to be such a shrewd Sandpiper or so bold. Let me be the first to say that, without any doubt in my mind, I accept the great Cheecheeshkishee as an equal. He and no other discovered the name of your daughter. He is very intelligent. I would be proud to have him as my friend. And for him to refuse your arrogant daughter sets him apart from all the others here. Because he doesn't like getting his feet wet makes him different from me, but no less of a bird."

Maang smiled, then continued, "I also refuse your daughter. There is much more to marriage than beauty. I am quite content with the woman I have. Your daughter, like you, is far too devious for me."

Beluga
Inuit legend

Here's a story about Creators love for all things.

I
t was a time when food was very scarce, even though it was Summer and
the ice was open. The seals and fish that the People relied upon were very
hard to find.

A young Inuit man had a strange Dream. During the dream, he was
told of a Creature that lived in the sea. He saw the Creature as pure white
and about the length of two People. It was a White Whale (Beluga). The
Dream told the young man where the whales could be located, and how to
hunt them.

In the morning, the young man went to the Elders and told them of
his Dream.

"It is a gift from Creator. Make all ready. We will hunt these creatures, as we have been advised," they said.

All was made ready and the kayaks were launched. Just as the Dream had promised, in exactly the place they had been directed, there swam many of the beautiful White Whales, frolicking among the cold ocean currents.

As the kayaks got near the Belugas, suddenly, a strange mist formed. The mist was not thick enough to terminate the hunt, and the Beluga gave themselves freely to the hunters. After taking only what they needed, the People returned to their village and gave thanks to the whales and Creator for the wonderful, life-giving presents they had been given.

Creator had given the Inuit a great gift, one of His very favorite Water People. But He could not watch the beautiful animals slaughtered, even though He knew His Inuit needed the flesh for food. So, as it is today when the People hunt the White Whale, Creator covers the area of the hunt with mist or clouds, so He does not have to watch His exquisite creations destroyed.

The Wolves that Wanted Fire
Coeur d'Alene legend

Why Wolves h*owl*.

I t was the middle of a hard Winter not long after the People were first given fire. The Wolves were cold, very hungry and envious. They would sit and stare longingly into the People's village, jealously watching its inhabitants warm themselves by their fire's glowing embers. The food the People cooked over their fires filled the air with delicious smells, heightening the Wolves' envy and causing saliva to drool constantly down their canine chins.

Finally, the Leader of the Wolves could stand the appetizing aromas no longer. He decided to send an emissary to beg for a spark from the People's fire so the Wolves would also have this wonderful gift. He purposely chose a pregnant female for the job but warned her, "When you approach the People of the village, go with humility. Go to them crawling on your belly or they might get frightened and kill you. Be submissive. You are pregnant and they will pity you." And so, the Wolf went into the village, advancing very slowly towards the fire where the People were gathered, crawling on her belly, wagging her tail and showing great respect.

The People were so pleased to see such a friendly Wolf that a great fuss was made of her. After they had finished stroking and petting her, they fed her delicious, cooked food, the like of which she had never tasted. But the thing that made her the happiest was they let her rest and then sleep by the warming fire.

The Wolf was so delighted by the treatment given her by her newfound friends that she forgot all about taking a spark from the fire back to the Leader of the Wolves. Instead, she settled down happily with the People and, a few days later, she had her pups. They, in turn, became the first domesticated Dogs.

It is said to this day that the reason Wolves howl is to show their displeasure, to complain. As we know, they never did get fire.

Killer Whale
Haida legend

A love story can take many forms.

It was Springtime and Eagle was sad because he was lonely. He needed something to cheer him up. What he really needed was a mate. Trust me, he had looked. He had examined every nook and cranny but to no avail. He seemed to be the only Eagle in his area.

One morning when the first rays of light were appearing in the East like spears piercing into the ripe Blackberry-colored Sky, turning it slowly into a grey-blue with just a hint of orange, Eagle sat perched amid the great beauty of the dawn. But he didn't care. He was fed up. He took off from his lonely aerie and headed out to sea. He had always enjoyed flying over the ocean where the strong Sea breezes would billow in his feathers, forcing him ever higher. Even this did not stir his heart as it had in the past. The ocean was beautifully clear that day and mirrored the reds and golds from Father Sun's rays.

Suddenly, Eagle's acute vision picked out something unusual below him—a dark shape swimming in the sea. He swooped down to investigate. The dark shape ghosted just beneath the surface was killer Whale.

In those days, Killer Whale was all one color—black. Eagle glided above the murky shape for some time. Then his loneliness got the better of him. He cried out to the Killer Whale below. The shape seemed to come closer to the surface. He cried out again. Sure enough, she responded.

As it turned out, Killer Whale was lonely, too. She had been looking for her own kind for many Round Moons but had found none. The cries she heard above stirred something in her soul and she thought, "What was that strange sound and who is making it?" She surfaced. Eagle was happy and he swooped lower, singing out his best songs as loud as he possibly could.

Whale felt a curious friendship toward Eagle and understood his powerful songs. They made her glad. She responded to Eagle by sending a plume of water from her spout. Eagle and Whale frolicked for hours until Father Sun found the center of the Sky. Then Eagle knew he must leave for he had not fed and it is dangerous for him not to eat regularly. He cried his good-byes, promising to return during the next Sun. Then sadly, he left his newfound friend.

Return to her he did, time and time again, spending most of his waking hours swooping and diving just above her. He brought her gifts of food, dropping the delicacies just in front of her. Much to her delight, as strange as it might sound, she was falling in love with him and he with her.

One day while Eagle flew above her, she made a decision. She swam quickly, diving deep. He, flying above, worried that something was wrong. When she had almost reached the ocean floor, she turned and headed towards the surface with as much speed as her mighty tail could provide. She shot from the Sea into the air. For a brief instant she was flying with her lover. At the peek of her ascent, their love was consummated and she fell back into the briny ocean.

It was some time later that an infant was born to Killer Whale, a strange child, one who had the power to fly through the air and had the voice of Eagle. Unlike its mother, it was black and white like its father. The very first Orca had been born to these unconventional lovers.

Dog-lover
Seneca legend

A story of bravery and devotion, this tale also describes the ultimate price of friendship.

A long time ago, there lived a Seneca man who was what we would today call a Dog lover. It was not that the other Seneca hated Dogs. But in those days, Dogs were mostly kept for hunting or to guard and warn the People of impending danger. They were working Animals and treated as such. The Seneca man we are talking about had three Dogs. All had names and were well fed and cared for. All three of his Dogs were allowed to sleep in his lodge. One in particular, Beaded Eyes, slept right with the warrior . . . mostly right on him. The Seneca Warrior loved his Dogs.

To describe Beaded-Eyes is not at all difficult. He was quite small, mostly white in color and had been given his name because of the two black markings around his eyes. He looked as though he was wearing a mask. Of all the Dogs, Beaded Eyes was definitely the young Warrior's favorite. The other two Dogs, both males, were respectively called Ugly and Big Skunk. Ugly had a huge head and scruffy, shaggy fur. He was not a good-looking Dog by any stretch of the imagination. Big Skunk was a black and white Dog that looked like a big Skunk. Luckily for the warrior, he usually did not smell like one.

The only problem the Warrior had with his Dogs was with Beaded Eyes, who had a lover called Lucky. Beaded Eyes would visit her—if you know what I mean by visit—as often as she would allow. The man who owned Lucky would complain about the visits. He was always throwing buckets of water over the amorous pair.

One day the young warrior was out hunting and, of course, he had his canine friends along with him. The Dogs ran here and there, sniffing at every scent they found, however old or new, with their tails wagging in exuberance at the very thought of the chase to come.

Beaded Eyes suddenly stopped dead in his tracks. Raising his head, he sniffed the air. Something was wrong. The warrior also halted, knowing Beaded Eyes had caught the scent of something dangerous as did the other two Dogs. Big Skunk lifted his head, also sniffing the air. Ugly let out a whimper. An eerie quiet settled over the forest. Even the birds fell silent. Something was very wrong.

All three Dogs walked slowly, stiff-legged toward their master. Not one was wagging its tail. In fact, their tails hung down between their legs. But the hair on the napes of their necks stood straight up.

The three Dogs stood by their master, all looking off into the bush at the unseen enemy. Beaded Eyes nuzzled the warrior's hand in an anxious manner, then returned his gaze to the same area of the bush as before. The young warrior studied the section of forest carefully while placing an arrow into his bow string. Nothing stirred, nothing unusual could be seen with the naked eye. But he, too, felt the presence of something very sinister.

Suddenly, a loud roar startled the Dogs and hunter back to reality. From the area the Dogs had scrutinized charged a huge Monster. It was probably a Sasquatch but as the young warrior had never seen one, he could not tell if it was or not. All he knew was it terrified him.

The Monster made a bee line towards the warrior. He let loose an arrow that flew true to the mark and hit the Beast but it didn't even slow the large, lumbering hulk down.

All three brave Dogs ran towards the Creature, barking and growling. They meant to do battle with the Beast. Ugly was the first to reach the oncoming Monster. He skidded to a halt, hackles bristling and fangs bared. The Monster stopped in its tracks, but only momentarily. It then took one swipe at the Dog and removed Ugly`s head in the process.

On seeing the power of the dreadful beast, the warrior called his remaining two Dogs back to his side. They ran towards him but so did the Monster.

The warrior turned tail and, as fast as his legs would carry him, he ran toward the safety of his village. All seemed to be going along well and his retreat appeared successful. He seemed to outrun the plodding Monster easily. Then, unexpectedly, he tripped over a root and fell heavily onto some rocks, knocking the wind from his body. The Dogs stopped and stood close at his side, wagging their tails but looking apprehensively back to where loud crashing and crunching sounds could be heard as the Monster smashed its way through the forest. The Dogs seemed to understand their master was in trouble.

He tried to get up but could put no pressure on one of his legs. The leg was broken and he immediately fell again. Both Dogs set off towards the oncoming Giant, seemingly understanding the warrior's predicament. Both were determined to save their master's life.

Big Skunk was the first to reach the beast. He circled it, snarling, his fangs exposed. The Sasquatch halted, swinging its huge arms at the snapping Dog. Big Skunk had learned from seeing his companion, Ugly, killed to stay out of reach. The Monster, with surprising speed, lunged forward, grabbing at the Dog. Big Skunk was snatched from the ground and flung through the air. His neck snapped. He was dead before his body hit the ground.

Brave little Beaded Eyes knew if his master's life was to be spared, he would have to somehow stop this terrible Ogre. His plan of action firmly in mind, Beaded Eyes ran at the Monster and jumped as high as his legs would propel him. He caught the creature by the throat and tore at it. The Monster let out a howl of rage, then another of pain as he ripped at the small Dog that was now hanging from his throat. But Beaded Eyes would not release the Monster and tightened his jaws even tighter. The creature yanked the little Dog away from its throat, at the same time tearing its own flesh. The Monster screamed with pain. Using both of his hands, he tore the tiny Dog to pieces. With a primal roar, he limped away, back to the Land he had come from, defeated and badly mutilated by the brave Beaded Eyes.

The young warrior crawled, pulling himself through the undergrowth toward his village. He was glad to be alive but realized his life had been saved by his three good companions. He finally dragged himself close enough to his encampment to call for help. The People came running to his aid and he was soon resting comfortably in his own lodge. While his leg was being set by the Medicine Man, he recounted his horrific tale.

After the story was finished, some of the warriors were so impressed with the bravery of the three Dogs they said they would go and bring the remains of the fearless Dogs back to the village for proper burial. "It would not be fitting to leave the bodies of such courageous creatures out in the bush," said one.

The next morning as Sun came up, the broken bodies of the three Dogs were blessed and a Prayer was said to help guide their Spirits into the next world after which their remains were laid to rest. After the Ceremony the young warrior thanked everyone for their help, kindness and understanding. He was then left alone for a time to reflect and remember the brave deeds that were done on the fateful day that the Monster came to the Land of the Seneca.

A short time later when his leg was well on the mend, a neighbor came to visit the young warrior.

"I thought you might like this," said the visitor as he opened his jacket and pulled from under it a small, furry object. He then placed it on the floor of the lodge. It was a puppy. "He was born to my Dog, Lucky. I know for sure that your Dog was the father." The little, white ball-of-fluff waddled over to where the young warrior sat. It sniffed around, then settled down on top of one of the young warrior's feet, looking happily up at him, wagging what was a poor excuse for a tail. Around the pup's eyes, were two, strange, black markings.

The young warrior was delighted. Beaded Eyes had returned.

Octopus and Raven
Nootka legend

In this story, we learn about the dangers of being annoying.

When the tide went out the Old People would come down to the beach and watch the Ocean retreat. One day as they watched, a young Octopus Woman came along carrying her basket on her back. Her hair was tied into eight, shiny, black braids. She was digging about in the sand, harvesting Clams. She found quite a lot.

Along came Raven, the Trickster, looking for someone to annoy. "What are you doing? Are you digging for Clams?" He asked.

Octopus didn't say anything as it was quite obvious to all what she was doing.

"What are you doing? Are you digging Clams?" insisted the irritating Raven.

"Go away, you silly Bird," was Octopus's direct answer.

Raven looked into her basket and said, "Any Clams in there?" grinning like an idiot at His own supposed humour. "Digging Clams are you? Eh, eh?"

It was quite obvious to the Old People who were watching that Octopus was getting annoyed. Suddenly, without warning, her eight, black, shiny braids came to life, four of them wrapping themselves around Raven's neck and the other four anchoring her to the beach. Raven thought her actions were in jest at first and carried on with His stupidity.

"Are you digging for Clams .... " he sarcastically asked. Now the braids gripped Raven's neck tighter, cutting off His foolish words. The exasperated Octopus replied to Raven's asinine question.

"Raven, let me tell You that I was digging for Clams. Are You listening to me? I was digging Clams," said the very annoyed Octopus, as she tightened her grip around Raven's throat, shaking Him a little. "Can You still hear me, Raven? I was digging for Clams. It was Clams that I was digging, you stupid, irritating, idiotic bird!"

The tide was coming back in now and it was starting to wash around Raven's feet. Octopus let her grip on Raven's neck loosen a little. Gasping for air, Raven pleaded, "Please let Me go, Octopus, My feet are getting wet, I was just being smart."

"Smart isn't a word I would have used for your absurd behavior," whispered Octopus as she tightened her grip once more around Raven's scrawny neck. Then, in a loud voice she continued, "I was digging Clams,

Raven. Can You comprehend?" The tide kept coming in and was soon lapping around Raven's belly. "I am answering Your question, Raven, I was digging for Clams." The water was now up to Raven's neck which was still being gripped tightly by Octopus's tentacles. Raven tried to communicate with Octopus but she held His throat so tightly that He could not.

The Old People could now only see the top of Raven's head and they worried Octopus would kill Raven. But just as the Ocean closed over Raven's head, Octopus released Raven and He flapped His way to the shore, a very bedraggled, soggy sight.

"I was digging Clams here," said Octopus, her voice bubbling to the surface of the Ocean.

Since that day, Raven has never asked Octopus another silly question, for He came to realize that silly questions can evoke hostile responses.

Porcupine
Plains Cree

Wisakachak, the Trickster, and sometimes Holy Man of the Cree, has great spiritual power. He can turn Himself into anything He wishes—a Woman, a Child, a Caribou, a Bird, anything, for He is one of Creator's helpers. This episode happened when He was asked by Creator, to make Mother Earth ready for the Human People.

The great orange ball slowly pulled free from the eastern edge of the World, causing the black night Sky to turn into the blues of the new day. Sun's first, soft rays of light pierced the forest canopy, dappling the floor below.

In unison, the Bird People sang their early morning praises to Creator and to Grandfather Sun. Wisakachak had already performed his Sunrise Ceremony but was happy to hear the Wing-Flappers do theirs.

It was the time before the Human People came. Wisakachak was here on Mother Earth to get all the Four-Leggeds, Water People, Wing-Flappers, Plant and Rock People ready for the coming of the Humans.

On this day, Wisakachak was walking through the bush, listening to the birds and thinking what a wonderful place Mother Earth was and how the Human People would enjoy life here as long as they lived with respect for Her.

Suddenly, Porcupine came running out of the bush just as fast as he could. Close on Porcupine's heels was Bear. In those days, Porcupine was not as he is today—he had no quills to defend himself. All he had was ordinary fur, just like Rabbit and Squirrel. The one thing Porcupine had lots of was enemies. They included Horned Owl, Bear, Wolf, Coyote, Lynx and Fisher. Porcupine had one staunch ally, namely a tree called Hawthorn.

Hawthorn had always protected Porcupine from predators. It did this with the aid of its needle-like thorns. It would allow Porcupine to pass through its branches but Bear it would not. All Bear got for his troubles this morning was a nose full of very painful spines.

Wisakachak watched the drama play out in front of him and felt sorry for Porcupine, knowing full well that for every Porcupine that was saved by Hawthorn, there were many less fortunate. In fact, Porcupine was on the verge of becoming extinct, he was so heavily hunted.

Wisakachak walked over to the Hawthorn tree and called out, "Little brother Porcupine, come down. I will do a trade with you. This is a trade that will be very beneficial to you and to the Human People to come."

Gingerly, Porcupine came down out of the tree to meet the Great Wisakachak of whom he had heard many things, not all of which were to Wisakachak's credit.

"I will give you a gift that will make it very difficult for the predatory animals to catch you," Wisakachak said, "I will give you the gift of the Hawthorn . . . the gift of sharp spines. I will put these spines all over your back and if you curl into a ball when attacked, you will not have to bother Brother Hawthorn again."

This arrangement sounded too good to be true to Porcupine because, as I have said, he had heard of Wisakachak's tricky personality.

"I would very much like to own this protection but what do you want from me for this wonderful gift?" asked Porcupine.

Wisakachak smiled knowingly, already suspecting Porcupine must have heard of his reputation and said, "You must promise you will give yourself freely to the Human People when they come. They will not take nearly as many of you as the beasts that hunt you now. These spines I will put on your back will be hollow, like the quills of the Bird People," explained Wisakachak. "The Human People will cut them into various lengths and use them as beads. They will dye them all sorts of colors and sew them onto their footwear and clothing. These People will be great artists. It will be an Honor for you to give them such beauty. As you will be Honored by those who receive your gift."

So it was that the wise Wisakachak made a good deal for both Porcupine and for the Human People to come.

Nowadays, it is only the most cunning of hunters, Fisher and the Human People who can easily catch Porcupine. Porcupine has been so grateful for his gift that he has readily given his quills to the Human People for their beautiful bead work. And because of Wisakachak's gift, there are many more Porcupines today.

Rattlesnake
Apache legend

This legend shows how survival sometimes depends on the ability to recognize danger. It's often used as a metaphor for addiction by illustrating the inherent risk of alcohol, drug and tobacco use.

There lived a very kind-hearted and thoughtful boy. One morning he was on his way to draw water for his mother from a nearby stream. He was about to dip his bucket into the mist- shrouded waters when he noticed a Rattlesnake lying on the bank close to the edge of the creek.

There had been a killing frost the night before and the snake had been caught in it and had become stiff with cold. The boy thought the snake dead and crouched down to examine it a little closer. Prodding it, first with a stick then, when it didn't move, gently pushing it with his foot. He was astonished when the snake spoke to him and he quickly jumped back.

"Young brother, do not fear me. Please help me. I need warmth or I will surely die. Please pick me up and hold me close to your body," it said in a soft, hissy, snake-like way.

"Not me," answered the boy. "If I pick you up, you will bite me."

"Why would you think that?"

"Because you are Rattlesnake!" exclaimed the boy, distrustful of the venomous creature.

"I could never bite someone who was helping me. Please rescue me. If I don't get warmth right now, I will die," said the snake in an even fainter, more pitiful voice.

The young boy thought over the request. Sympathizing with the reptile's plight, he decided to help it. He picked up the rigid snake and held it close to his body, warming its almost frozen flesh. The snake gradually revived and started to wriggle about. Suddenly, it raised its flat head and struck at the boy, who dropped it immediately shouting, "You said you wouldn't bite me if I helped you?"

"Yes, but when you picked me up, you knew I was Rattlesnake," sneered the snake as it slithered off.

The Ugly People
Cherokee legend

While the Sun is male to most Native Peoples of North American, to the Cherokee People, Sun is female.

Sun was very selfish and conceited. She, in Her wisdom, decided that She wanted a baby. The only male powerful enough to give Her that child was Moon. But He lived on the other side of Mother Earth. There were a few times Sun and Moon would share the same Sky and it was on those occasions, that Sun would court Moon. Moon was flattered by Sun's attentions and believed, in His heart, that She had fallen in love with Him. Not long after this, according to Cherokee history a strange phenomenon happened—the Day became as Night.

Sun had lured Moon into a position where She could mate with Him. It was an eclipse, a very special eclipse, one that would bring a daughter into the life of Sun. Unfortunately for Moon, when His task was done, arrogant

Sun would have nothing more to do with Him, save for those few days where the two would share the Sky at dawn or dusk.

Even though Sun was a very selfish woman, She doted on Her child. She would take the little one everywhere She went. She spoiled her, and smothered her with love so much so, that the child grew precocious and more like her Mother every day. But later, in her teens, she became independent and thoughtful, more like her Father, with whom she longed for a better relationship. On the few times she talked to her Father she found Him to be very wise and thoughtful, tolerant of all and totally unlike her Mother. Moon taught her about the ways of the Cherokee and the animals and birds of Mother Earth. She loved to watch the World below and the People and animals on it. Most of all, she loved the birds and their great beauty.

Sun grew very jealous of her daughter's friendship with Moon and of her liking for the People, animals and birds that lived on Earth. But interfering with Her daughter's relationship with Moon just made Her daughter appreciate her Father more and her Mother less.

As soon as she was old enough to fend for herself, daughter Sun moved out from her Mother's home and built her own Lodge in the center of the Sky. She lived happily there but to her chagrin, her mother visited her each and every day. It wasn't that she did not love her Mother, but every day?

Mother Sun would rise in the East and set off toward the center of the Sky. When She reached Her daughter's Lodge, She would go in and visit with her. Then, Mother Sun would return to the East instead of continuing on Her normal path and setting in the West. Moon would reign during the time in which She rested, at night.

Of course, the People noticed the change in Sun's patterns and became concerned as the middle of the day was now much hotter than ever before. Their crops of beans and corn suffered. The People would stop what they were doing and squint up at the bright object in the center of the Sky. They all hoped everything would return too normal soon.

On one particular visit from her Mother, Sun's daughter was telling Her about how she had been watching the People below and she believed that there was something wrong.

"Come Mother, let me show You," she led her Mother outside of the lodge and pointed down to the Earth below. It had been a long time since Mother Sun had looked down to see how the People below were doing. She had been too busy with Her daughter. She really didn't want to look but She did finally take a peek. What She saw were the People looking up at Her, their half-closed eyes shaded with their hands, trying to see what was wrong in the Heavens above.

"The Earth People are so rude and so ugly. They have such squinty kinds of looks. They are always screwing up their faces and have silly grins all over them, "She thought. Then She took another look and there below were more of the People staring up at Her, making what She considered impolite faces at Her.

One morning when Mother Sun and Father Moon shared the Sky, Sun asked Moon what He thought of these ugly, impudent People.

"On the whole," He said, "Earth People are quite handsome. I certainly don't think they are being impertinent to You. I think You are overreacting after not looking at them for so long. You have been so busy with Our child," said Moon.

But in the days to come, the more Mother Sun looked down at the People, the more angry She became. While having lunch with Her daughter, Mother Sun complained bitterly, "These People will never look directly at Me and even when they try, they always make ugly faces at Me. They are very rude. I have had just about all I can stand of them."

Her daughter did not agree and sided with her father Moon saying, "I think it is Your imagination Mother. They are handsome People with kindness in their hearts. I love all the Earth Peoples, the animals and the beautiful birds."

"Well, I hate them, birds and all. I'm going to kill them off. They're just too ugly and rude to stomach," said Mother Sun. She left Her daughter's lodge in the middle of the Sky but instead of heading back to the East, She stayed in the center of the Sky, shining down Her powerful rays. "Look at those idiots below looking at Me, screwing up those silly faces. Well, I'll show them," and She did.

A short time later, a Council was held among the Elders of the Cherokee. They prayed to Creator for help to solve the dispute between Mother Sun and themselves and they wondered what they had done to deserve such terrible treatment.

It had grown extremely hot and unbearably humid as Mother Sun's rays dragged every drop of water into the atmosphere. The air hung like a soggy curtain. Mother Sun beat down on the Cherokee Lands unmercifully. Another Council was held, one of the oldest and wisest Elders said, "The only thing to do is to kill or capture Mother Sun's child, maybe then She will get back to Her old self."

It was well known to the Cherokee that Rattlesnake knew a secret path to the Sky and if anyone could kill Sun's daughter, he could. But Rattlesnake refused. He loved the heat.

As time went on, Sun continued to beat down unmercifully. Now the humidity was gone. It became so hot it dried up most of the rivers and lakes. The game and fish the People relied upon died off by the millions. Then the People started to die by the thousands. It is said half of all the Cherokee People had died before they finally decided to go for help. Again the Cherokee sent emissaries to get help from Rattlesnake and this time he agreed.

Rattlesnake set off to the Sun's daughter's lodge by his secret route. Upon reaching his destination, he coiled up outside the daughter's lodge and awaited his chance. Soon, someone stirred in the lodge. Rattlesnake got ready. A soft, shimmering light came to the door of the lodge. And as Mother Sun's daughter emerged, Rattlesnake reared back and struck with its mortally wounding bite. Since that time, the Cherokee revere Rattlesnake, because, he killed their enemy. And, to this day, as long as it is left alone, Rattlesnake will not attack his friends, the Cherokee People.

Mother Sun went to the Lodge to visit Her daughter and there She discovered Her daughter's lifeless body. With great sorrow and tears, She lifted up daughter Sun in a tender embrace.

"Who would do such a thing?" She cried. She looked down at Earth. There were no People to be seen. "Where are they? They must be hiding." Then it dawned on Her. "It was the Cherokee, the Ugly Ones, they have retaliated for the drought I caused. They have killed My daughter." At first She was angry, but then anger gave away again to sadness. Broken hearted, She went back into the lodge and sobbed, promising Herself never to come out again.

The Land of the Cherokee was now dark but at least the People stopped dying from the heat. However, the food supply had become so critical they were still starving to death. It was night all the time and the People that were left alive were in fear of drowning from the deluge of tears emanating from Sun's eyes.

The Cherokee Leaders were at their wits end, they did not know what to do. Finally, they went to the Little People and begged for help. First they asked the Little People why Sun was doing what She was doing.

"She thinks that you are being rude to Her, because you make funny faces at Her. She thinks you are all very ugly."

"Rude? We are not rude People and ugly! Well, we must admit there are a few among our People who are not as handsome as others but on the whole, we are a good-looking People."

The Little People told the Cherokee the only thing that would appease Mother Sun would be the return of Her daughter.

"But Rattlesnake has killed her," said one of the Cherokee emissaries.

"Then you must travel to the Land of the Dead and bring her Spirit back," said the Leader of the Little People. "We will tell you how this can be done."

Seven Cherokee men were chosen to go to the Land of the Dead and bring the soul of the Sun's daughter back with them. The Little People gave each man a rod made from Sacred wood and then crafted a very special box to put the Spirit in. They instructed the seven warriors how it was to be done. They also cautioned them that after the Spirit had been placed in the box, they should not open it under any pretext, until reaching their home, the Land of the Cherokee.

The seven warriors traveled for seven days into the West. Finally, they found the Land of the Dead. They were very frightened but in fact, the Dead People they found there were dancing and seemed to be having a good time. The warriors did as they were told and made a circle around the dancers and waited for Sun's daughter to pass them. When she did, they touched her with the Sacred rods they had been given by the Little People. When the last of the seven warriors touched her, she fell over as if dead again. But the Little People had told them, she would actually be alive and would be able to return to her Mother. They quickly put her into the box and carried her away, back toward their home. The other Spirits didn't seem to care. They just kept on dancing.

As they carried Sun's daughter home, she started to say things to them. "I am very hungry," she pleaded, "Could you please feed me?" The warriors knew it was a trick.

Again she cried out. "I am very thirsty would you give me a drink." Still, the warriors remembered the Little People's instruction and refused her.

When they were nearly home, they heard daughter Sun speak out in a very weak voice, "I am suffocating in here. I am dying." Then all went very quiet.

At first, the warriors thought the Spirit was trying to fool them again. But when they heard nothing from the box for half a day they began to worry that they had killed the newly revived ghost.

"Perhaps, we should open the lid just a little and peek inside, to see if she is all right."

As they cracked the box open, a beautiful Redbird shot out and flew away. To this day, we know Cardinal is the Sun's daughter and because the seven warriors did not do as the Little People had told them, the Cherokee cannot go to the Land of the Dead to bring back Spirits.

Moon told Sun what had happened, and She was even more upset. She vowed never to come out of Her lodge again. She cried and cried, causing the darkened Lands to flood.

The Cherokee held another Council. It was decided that to prove once and for all they were not Ugly People and that they loved Mother Sun, they would hold a dance in honor of Her. They selected the most handsome men and women who put on their finest clothes, and they danced and sang for Mother Sun.

Mother Sun would not come out of Her daughter's Lodge, but She did stop crying and listened to the fine songs the People sang. A little while later She ventured a peek from the door of Her lodge to see who was doing the fine singing. As She looked down from inside the doorway of Her Lodge, Her sad, soft rays shone on the People below. The Cherokee were able to look up without squinting, She saw that, indeed, as the Moon and Her daughter had told Her, these were fine-looking People not at all ugly as She had thought.

She took pity on them, deciding Her war with them had gone on long enough. She made up Her mind to shine at Her brightest only at midday, and to move around the Sky like She used to instead of sitting in the middle. From that day on She has risen in the East and set in the West, becoming a friend to the fine-looking People below. When She got over Her grief, She realized that all Her hate for the Cherokee had been a misunderstanding and that misunderstanding had caused Her and the People great heartache.

Mother Sun was glad Her Beautiful daughter had been brought back from the Land of the Dead to become what she truly loved—a bird, the Cardinal—and now lived with the handsome People.

Sun went back to Her old ways. From then on, She has remained a good friend to the Cherokee. However, it is said the next time the day becomes night She may try again for another child with Her friend and lover—Moon.

The Floating Island
Mi'kmaq legend

How Christianity came to the Mi'kmaq.

Not so long ago, just before the White Man came, a young woman had a very strange Dream. She Dreamed a small island came floating toward the Land of the Mi'kmaq. On this island were a lot of Bears, shaking thin trees.

When she awoke from her unusual Dream, she went immediately to the Medicine Man and told him of the Dream. She asked him its meaning, but he did not understand the Dream and had no answers for her. She was very confused.

The next night she had the same strange Dream. Very disturbed over this second Vision, she got up and went for a walk to think things over, trying to make sense of her premonition.

The first light of day, found her walking along the beach near her village. She noticed something unusual, way out to sea—it was the island she had seen in her dream. Indeed, the island was floating toward the shore on which she stood. She could plainly see the thin trees, waving about at the edges of the island. But, she couldn't make out what was causing them to shake.

She ran quickly to tell of her sighting and to tell the Medicine Man her Dream seemed to be coming true. On hearing of the bizarre phenomenon, the Warriors grabbed their weapons and ran speedily to the beach. The island was now a lot closer and the People gathered on the shore could clearly see what the young woman had thought were Bears waving poles were actually men, strange men with hairy faces who were dressed in dark furs, making them resemble bears.

Soon, the Mi'kmaq realized the island was a very large canoe, and the tree-poles were being used as paddles to propel the island craft through the water. In the midst of the Bear-like men stood another man, unlike the hairy men. He was dressed in white, flowing robes.

The odd canoe beached and the man in the white robes came toward the gathered Native People. He carried in front of him the symbol of a cross and spoke in a strange language, one the Mi'kmaq could not understand.

The warriors drew their bows and were about to kill the white-robed stranger when the Medicine Man stepped forward and asked the young woman, "Is this the island you saw in your Dream?"

"Yes," answered the girl.

The Medicine Man shouted to the gathered warriors, "This man is not to be killed. He is to be Honored. His coming was predicted in a dream, given to a young woman of our Tribe."

And so it was the Mi'kmaq let the man in white stay among them. Soon, he had learned the Mi'kmaq language and began teaching the People about the ways of his God.

Even though the Elders and the Medicine Man spoke against it, many Mi'kmaq soon adopted the new religion and took it for their own.

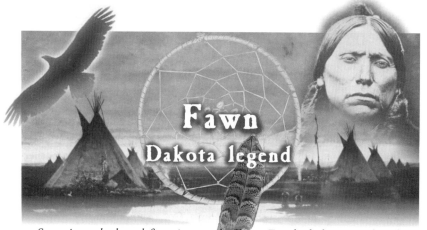

Fawn
Dakota legend

Sometimes the best defense is a good offense. For the baby Deer, though, blending in is the key to survival.

Creator made all the animals and to each He gave gifts—to Fox, He gave great cunning and stealth; to Raven, flight and curiosity; to Duck, flight and the ability to swim; and to the slow and cumbersome Animal like Porcupine, He gave quills for protection. To Deer and Rabbit, He gave great speed. But to the young of the Deer, the fawns, He gave no special abilities or defense. He gave them no burrow, no camouflage, no sharp teeth or claws—Creator had left the fawn defenseless.

One Spring after the Deer had delivered their young, one doting mother almost lost her baby. This is what happened. Coyote, who was always hungry, was prowling around the herd, looking for any young that had strayed from their mothers' side. Down wind from the herd, peering from the dense, forest undergrowth at the clearing where the Deer grazed, he spotted a very small, defenseless, wobbly-legged youngster standing some distance from the main body of animals. Creeping slowly and stealthily through the vegetation, Coyote got within a few strides of the baby. With a great rush he descended on the defenseless fawn. The youngster's mother, who was grazing nearby, saw the commotion and raced toward Coyote, her mother's love giving her the bravery needed to fend off the hungry Coyote. Putting her own life in great danger, head down, snorting with rage, the young mother butted Coyote, knocking him, hitting him so hard He suddenly lost his appetite. He slunk away to find easier prey.

After saving her baby's life, the young mother was very frightened and shaken. Once she calmed down, she got quite angry and decided that she would beseech Creator (Wakan Tanka) to help her baby and all fawns protect themselves in some way.

"Creator," she prayed, "my young child has no defense whatsoever. She is so young she cannot even walk properly. Please do something to help all our young ones."

Creator saw the young mother's plight and answered, "Take this pretty child into the forest, I will do something to help."

The young mother walked with her baby into the forest. Under the trees, the bright Sun, shining through the forest's canopy, dappled the youngster's body, making it appear to have spots. Creator appeared before the pair and ran

His hands over the body of the fawn. From that day to this one, the dappled spots have remained on the fawn up until it becomes an adult. However, Creator was not finished. He leaned down to the fawn and took a deep breath, swallowing all scent the youngster had.

"From this time forth the young of Deer will not only have this dappled pattern to disguise them but they will not carry a scent," he explained. "Their enemies will not be able to detect them."

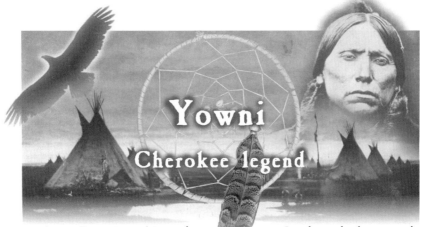

Yowni

Cherokee legend

Many First Nations' Legends connect Bears to People, and a large number of them tell of how People became Bears. There are still Native hunters who will not kill Bear. They say "If Bear is hurt, it will cry out with a Human voice. People and Bear are one."

The population had grown so dramatically that the village had become dangerously overcrowded. The soil had grown poor with over use. The corn and beans the People grew were not yielding enough to feed everyone. Overhunting close to the village had made game scarce. The People had to go on longer and longer trips to find meat. People often went hungry, but still the population grew.

In one crowded, bustling village a lot of People had become ill with unfamiliar maladies. Amongst all of this lived one very sickly young boy who most villagers thought would not last another Winter. One night, the feeble young boy had a strange Dream. An exotic Spirit Animal came to him in the Dream, the likes of which he had never before seen. The Spirit Animal was covered with hair and, although it was a Four-Legged, it stood on two and spoke to the boy.

"I have been sent to help you. To Creator, you are a very special boy. If you do as I say, you will become well. All illness will leave your body. You will become stronger than any of your People have ever been. But to obtain this prowess and strength, you must follow my instructions. This is what you have to do. First, you must fast for seven days so your mind and heart will become clear. After your fast, leave the village and go to live deep in the mountains. It is there you will find your true destiny. I will remain your Spirit Animal. I will always guide you. I will come to you in your Dreams. You will become something very special." The Dream then faded.

The next morning, the boy excitedly told his parents about his Dream and that he wished to comply with the Spirit's wishes. His parents, of course, tried to dissuade the boy because of his ill health. Then, his father. relenting somewhat, whispered sadly to his wife. "He will not be with us long, my wife. We should respect his wishes. They may be his last."

Food was very scarce, so it was easy for the boy to abstain from it. As instructed he fasted for seven days, taking only water for sustenance. You would have thought that fasting for such a length of time would weaken the already ill boy. In fact, each day he seemed to get a little better and a little stronger. On the eighth day he left the village feeling quite weak but strangely renewed and revitalized. It was as though his sickness had left him.

The ravenous boy set off towards the mountains. On his trek he ate only wild food—berries, fruit and small animals such as Frogs and Squirrels. He cooked nothing and found it tasted better. After many Suns of travelling, he was in the heart of the mountains, still hunting and foraging to feed himself. It was now late summer and there was a lot of fruit which he consumed in great quantities. Later, when the fruit was finished, he once again lived off small game. Still, he cooked none of the food he ate and was by now convinced it tasted much better than cooked food.

Unlike the village where he used to live, food was abundant. As the Moons passed he grew stronger. The Spirit Animal came to the boy frequently in his Dreams and instructed him in survival, fishing and hunting skills. The Spirit told him of all the bird, animal and fish migrations and how best to catch them. The boy learned well.

During the following Spring, the boy returned to his village to visit his family. He brought much food with him. His family feasted. They were very glad to see how strong and healthy their son had become but were shocked to see that he had long, brown hair growing from his body. The nails on his hands and feet were longer and his shoulders stooped as if he was prematurely aging.

"You have the appearance of a very old man," said his mother. "And yet, I can tell you are very healthy and now possess great strength. What has caused your body to change in such a manner?"

"I am not sure," he answered. "But I think my change of diet has something to do with the new hair and the way I have physically changed. You see, I do not cook any of my food. I eat everything raw." He hesitated, then smiled wryly saying "At least with this extra hair I stay warmer in the Winter." The boy went on to tell his parents how easy it was for him to find food. "Even when it snows, the animals and birds give themselves freely to me. When the ground thaws, there are all kinds of roots that can be dug for."

His parents told him life in the village was even worse now than when he had left. The lack of food and overcrowding had caused tension and frayed nerves. There had even been a murder. . . something which had never happened before. The family sat long into the night, discussing the boy's new life and how sad village life had become.

"Then you must join me out in the mountains," said the boy. His parents readily agreed. He hesitated before continuing, "But if you do wish to join me, I think you should fast in the same manner that I did. I feel we will achieve something special if we follow my Spirit Animal's requests."

They agreed they would leave the village with their son and they would follow the Spirit's requests. Soon, the whole family was gathering—children, aunts, uncles, all their close relatives. Together, they fasted for seven days. They then set out for the mountains to start their new lives where they adopted the same feeding habits as the boy. They never cooked anything. Soon, they, too, were growing hair on their bodies and their body shapes were changing.

Back at their former village the family had been very well liked and were missed by all. At a meeting of the Elders, it was decided to send an emissary to find the family in the mountains and to ask them to return to the village to be reunited with their friends.

The emissary, on finding the family, was surprised by their high spirits and good health, but was shocked to see that they had all grown long, brown hair over their entire bodies. The young boy was the strangest sight. He now walked mostly on all fours and seemed to be the Leader of the family. He had grown enormously. One could tell at a glance that he had the strength of many People. The emissary sat with the family and told them of the Elders' request that the family return to their village.

"We cannot do that," said the boy. "Creator has changed us. We are not as we were. We have become as the Spirit Animal who guides me. We are Yowni (Bear). We are a new form of animal that will be strong Medicine for the Cherokee. We know it has become very difficult for the hunters to feed all the People who live in the village, so we will even give our own flesh to you in order that the People may become stronger. However, a man who hunts Yowni must first sing 'The Bear Song.'" The boy then taught the emissary the song. "He must fast from morning till evening. He will sing the song as he leaves camp but he must never sing the song twice in the same day. If he does all these things in a Sacred Manner, we will come to him and he may take our flesh. After our deaths, we must be cut into four pieces. When he has butchered our meat, he must cover the area with leaves where it was done. Then the hunter may depart with our flesh. But he must look back while he can still see the spot where he killed Yowni."

The emissary left the family to report his bizarre findings to the Elders. Just before he got out of sight, he stopped and looked back and saw the whole Yowni family were now walking on all fours.

When he arrived back in his home village, the People still hungered. Some time later, a brave hunter who had learned "The Bear Song" went to the mountains where everything the young boy had told the emissary came true. He easily found Yowni. It was as if Bear knew his fate. It was almost too easy for the hunter to kill the animal.

After the hunter had butchered the meat, he did as instructed and covered the bloody area with leaves where the animal had fallen. Feeling sad about the loss of such a wonderful-looking animal, he set off for the village. After walking a short distance and while still in sight of where the leaves were piled high on the remains of the dead Bear, he turned to take a last look. He wasn't positive but he thought he saw the leaves move ever so slightly. Then, the ground began to tremble. Up through the leaves rose a magnificent Bear. Yowni shook itself free from clinging leaves, looked towards the hunter and then lumbered back into the bush. The hunter was exhilarated and gave thanks to Great Spirit.

And so it was that the Spirit Animal had told the truth. The boy and his family had been given a great gift. Yowni have been admired ever since that time for their great strength and courage by the Cherokee. It is well known that the outcome of the match can be very different from the one described if a hunter does not pursue Yowni in the Sacred Manner.

Wind Eagle
Abnaki legend

Gluscabi, also known as Glooskap, is a hero and Trickster according to the folklore of the Abnaki Confederation. It is said He created Himself with some leftover, magic dust Creator had let fall to Earth. This ever-young Warrior is much like Wisakachak of the Cree in that He is always looking for adventure but not always getting things quite right. He lives with His mentor, a wise, old Woodchuck who He adopted as His Grandmother. His stories are told as much as teaching tools as they are for entertainment.

Gluscabi pushed His canoe out from the bank and hopped into it. He began stroking vigorously, dipping deeply and pulling the paddle with His great strength, powering the small boat through the rough water, towards a fairly large island that sat not far from shore. He knew a large number of ducks always congregated on the island. As He pulled His small craft out beyond the cover of the bay and out into the open waters, the lake became quite turbulent. Soon, the waves were pitching His little boat about quite ferociously.

In those days, the wind blew constantly over the Land and waters of the Abnaki. But sometimes it blew harder than others and this was obviously one of those days. The wind had become a head wind. It was so strong that, even with His vigorous, powerful paddling Gluscabi was getting nowhere. A gale-force wind was now blowing and it would take a full day to travel the short distance to the island at the rate He was moving. Disgusted and disheartened, Gluscabi finally gave up, turned His canoe around and was quickly blown back to the shore where He had started.

Very annoyed, He took His hunting implements from the canoe and angrily stomped off towards home. Later that evening, after He had eaten His supper, He began complaining to His adopted Grandmother. "Grandmother Woodchuck, this constant wind is too much. Today, it was so strong I couldn't get out to the island to hunt ducks. What causes the wind to blow all the time and why does it sometimes blow so hard?"

"It is the Wind Eagle, My Grandson. It is his job to cause the wind to blow," she answered. "Without the wind, our People would get sick. The wind makes us strong. It blows away the bad smells."

"Why does it blow all the time. Can't this bird give us a break? I don't know what strength and wind have to do with each other. Where does this Wind Eagle live?"

"He lives in the . . . " she hesitated. "Why do You wish to know? What are You planning, Gluscabi? Please don't interfere with the order of things. When You do, many things go wrong."

"Grandmother, you do me an injustice. I would not harm the Wind Eagle. Where does it live?" He pressed.

"I cannot tell You, I don't think You should know. I beg You, Gluscabi, don't interfere with things. Leave them the way they are meant to be."

Gluscabi realized the information He needed was not forthcoming from Grandmother Woodchuck, so He excused himself and took out His blanket and got ready to go to sleep, all the time formulating a plan to find and subdue this very annoying Windmaker.

Early the next morning, Gluscabi got up, His plan set firmly in His mind. He took a stout rope and set off on His Stop-The-Wind-Eagle-From-Doing-What-It's-Doing Quest. Always facing into the wind, He walked, knowing full well if He did this, eventually, He would meet up with the aggravating bird who caused the wind to blow. He walked for many days with the wind gradually becoming stronger. "I must be nearing its lair," thought Gluscabi. Just as He had this notion, a huge gust came along and ripped all the clothes from His body. Away they flew like dancing leaves in a breeze.

"Wait until I get my hands on you, My Fine, Feathered Friend. I'll give you wind all right," mumbled the disgruntled, naked Gluscabi.

The next day He spied a mountain way off in the distance. Nothing seemed to be growing on it. "Probably, the Eagle has blown it all away," thought Gluscabi. As He neared the mountain, the wind was so strong His hair was now being blown straight out behind Him. He pressed on toward the source of the ever-blustering gale. "I think the Wind Eagle will be somewhere near the top of that mountain," He said to Himself.

As He reached the foot of the mountain, the wind became even stronger, it was very difficult for Gluscabi to walk upright. He had to hold onto rocks and pull Himself forward. Suddenly, a mighty gust of wind came up with such power that His long, jet black hair was ripped from His head, causing Him much pain and further distressing the already very annoyed, naked, young man.

The last straw came shortly afterwards, as Gluscabi scrambled ever nearer to the source of the wind. The Wind Eagle's constant wing-beating caused Gluscabi's eyebrows to be whisked from His face by an all-powerful blast. At last, He could see the bird. It was not as large as He had imagined, but it was bigger than ordinary Eagles. It was perched just below the top of the mountain, constantly flapping its wings, beating the air into a wild, frenzied, gale-force wind.

"Greetings," shouted Gluscabi, hanging on for dear life to a large rock.

"Who is there?" squawked the Wind Eagle, squinting at Gluscabi with its beady eyes.

"My name is Gluscabi. Stop beating your wings for a moment and I will tell you something that might help you," said Gluscabi, while thinking to Himself that He would like to wring the wretched creature's neck.

Wind Eagle slowed down the flapping but didn't entirely stop. He peered suspiciously at Gluscabi. "What do You want to tell me?" he asked

"Firstly, that you are doing a fine job of wind-making. You know, if you were doing this job from the summit of this mountain, you would cause an even stronger wind to blow!"

The Wind Eagle stopped flapping his wings and sat and thought over Gluscabi's suggestion. "This may be true, Young Man, but I'm afraid I can no longer fly or even walk for that matter. I have been causing the wind to blow for so many years I have lost the art of either of those two simple things. So you see, even if I wanted to, I couldn't get there."

"Don't worry about that, I will carry you to the summit. It's the least I can do. In fact, I have brought a good stout rope with Me and I will make a harness for you and convey you to the top of this mountain where you can start up your wind business once more."

Gluscabi quickly made a harness and bound it to the Eagle's wings, pressing them tightly to its body. He then hoisted the Wind Eagle up onto His back and struggled with the heavy beast towards the summit.

Of course, Gluscabi never had any intention of carrying out His promise to the Wind Eagle. As soon as He came to a convenient crevice, He dropped Wind Eagle into the fissure and then pushed him deeper with His foot, wedging the bound, hapless bird firmly in between the two rock faces. Feeling very proud of Himself, Gluscabi quickly returned to the Land of the Abnaki, where Sun now shone and the wind was gone. The pesky bird had been defeated.

Gluscabi was happy. He went on several, successful, duck hunts and sat around, basking in the warm, windless weather. His hair and eyebrows were soon growing back. Shortly after, with Sun's heat constantly beating down and no wind to cool one down, it became too hot to sit outside, and things began to smell bad. Even the lake got a sort of brown scum on it, and the fish began to die mysteriously. Their bodies floated to the top of the water and, soon, their rotting flesh caused the air to smell even more putrid. Hunting and fishing became all but impossible in this smelly region.

One evening, while sitting by their campfire, Grandmother Woodchuck asked, "Gluscabi, have You anything to do with this predicament the Abnaki find themselves in?"

"What predicament, Grandmother?" asked a supposedly surprised Gluscabi.

"The lack of wind! This heat wave! Did You visit the Wind Eagle and do something bad to it even though I begged You not to?"

Gluscabi looked at His feet, then at the lake but never directly into Grandmother Woodchuck's eyes. Without ever getting an answer but knowing in her heart that He was the culprit, she continued, "Go quickly, Gluscabi. Set right the wrongs You have done." She shook her head, amazed at how stupid a bright, clever person like Gluscabi could sometimes be.

Gluscabi, knowing He must make amends, hurried back to the Wind Eagle's mountain. He went up to the spot where He had wedged the unfortunate bird. He found him where He had left him. Peering down at the trapped bird, He said, "What seems to be the problem?"

"Who's there?" squawked Wind Eagle.

"It's Glus . . . " He quickly cut Himself off, remembering that He had told the Wind Eagle His name last time. "Perhaps he won't recognize Me," Gluscabi thought, then continued by saying, "It's a young man from the Lands of the Abnaki. Odzihozo is what I am called. I have come to see why the wind no longer blows. Who has done this terrible thing to you?" asked Gluscabi, pulling the Eagle free from the crevice.

"It was a really ugly Young Man that put me here. He had no hair on His head nor eyebrows on His face and He was as naked as a jaybird. He told me He would carry me to the summit of this mountain. Instead, the obnoxious, young devil shoved me into this crevice," said the big Eagle, preening its ruffled feathers.

"I am sorry you have been abused this way. Now that I have liberated you from your captivity, I will carry you to the place where the unpleasant young man promised to take you."

"What a fine boy You are; not at all like that Dog dropping who came here with the sole intent of stopping my wind-making assignment," said the thankful but duped bird.

And so it was that Gluscabi carried the grateful Eagle to the summit of the mountain and undid his bonds. "Wind Eagle, before you start up again, can I ask you to do something for me?"

Wind Eagle replied, "Of course You can, Young Man. I owe You my life. Had You not come along, I might have starved to death. What is it You wish?"

"Well, instead of blowing all the time, why don't you take some breaks? Blow for a few days, then rest for a few; then blow hard for a day or two, then rest again."

"What a good idea. Why, I could learn to fly again on my days off. I will do as You suggest, Odzihozo. What a grand idea."

And so it is that the Wind Eagle does not blow constant breezes anymore. We now have a more varied pattern and all is in balance, all because of a wise, old Woodchuck and her adopted Grandson, Gluscabi, or should I say Odzihozo ....

Owl
Cree legend

This Wisakachak episode happened when He was asked by Creator, after the devastation of the Great Flood, to recreate some of the Animals and Birds and invent some brand new ones.

Wisakachak had been really busy inventing. He was tired and irritable as He had not had much sleep lately on account of all of His recreating. He had already made a lot of the creatures that now inhabit the Earth, and was, at this point, making the first Rabbit and had just finished breathing life into him.

"How do you like yourself?" asked Wisakachak of the newly formed animal. Rabbit looked down at himself and said, "I think I look pretty good. Thank you. Am I going to need to run fast?"

"Yes, you probably are. There are a lot of animals that will definitely want to eat you," advised Wisakachak.

"Oh, dear, then, I had better have longer legs. I think they would be better to run on."

"Then that's what you shall have," smiled Wisakachak amiably.

From off to one side came the voice of grumpy old Owl who was sitting, watching the proceedings, "How come he gets to order what he wants? You never asked me if I wanted extra things."

Wisakachak said in a disgruntled voice, "Go away, Owl, I'm very busy and very tired. You should know better than to disturb Me when I'm working."

Owl disregarded Wisakachak's request and continued, "Nobody asked me when I was made if I would like some alterations. I would have liked nice, red plumage .... "

"I warn you for the last time. No more silly comments," said Wisakachak angrily.

"Don't threaten me," said Owl haughtily. "What about Blue Jay? He has beautiful feathers. Was I ever asked if I wanted .... "

Bang—down came Wisakachak's fist, right on top of Owl's head. The sudden turn of events was a crude interruption of his monologue and a shortening of his neck. It also pushed his head down into his body, making him look as he does today—like a bird without a neck.

"Ouch," screeched Owl, "You didn't have to do that ... ouch, my neck hurts. I think it's broken."

"I warned you, Owl. I will not put up with any more of your nonsense. Now, either go away or sit and keep quiet," said Wisakachak.

Wisakachak turned back to Rabbit and started pulling on his back legs, making them longer.

"There, that should make you a lot faster. With those big back legs, you will be able to spring through the air with great speed. Anything else?"

"Yes," said Rabbit, "I would like really good hearing."

"And so you will have it, My Friend," said Wisakachak, pulling on Rabbit's ears and making them as they appear today. The length greatly improved his hearing.

Owl, whose neck was still throbbing with pain was, as ordered, sitting quietly watching the goings on—at least up until this point. But the time came when he just couldn't help but chime in again. When he saw Rabbit getting his ears lengthened, he squawked, "Nobody ever asked me if I wanted better hearing when I was created. I don't think you like me."

"I am warning you for the last time, Owl. Don't interrupt Me," admonished an angry Wisakachak.

"I can and will say whatever I want. Nobody asked me ...."

Which was as far as Owl got. Wisakachak turned again, picking him up with one hand and with the other, plucking up two feathery tufts, one on either side of Owl's head. The tufts resembled ears.

"Ouch," squawked Owl as one tuft got tugged up. "Ouch, ouch," he hooted upon the other being pulled into place.

"There, Owl, now you have ears. I must say, you look very attractive. I hope it hurts," said Wisakachak sardonically as He turned His attentions once again towards Rabbit.

"Ouch, my head hurts," screeched Owl, hopping around in agony.

"Tell someone who cares! Go away, Owl. I don't want to hear another hoot out of you. And I do mean—GO AWAY," shouted the very annoyed Wisakachak, again turning back to concentrate on Rabbit.

"Now, Rabbit, is there anything else?" asked Wisakachak gruffly.

"Ouch, oh, gee," Owl persisted.

Wisakachak was furious. He shook His head, leaving Rabbit's side one last time, saying, "I told you to go away. I warned you. You don't seem to take advice very well." He grabbed Owl. Owl knew he'd gone too far. He was terrified.

"You seem a little upset, Wisakachak. I'm sorry," Owl whispered. It was too late for apologies. Owl's eyes got wider and wider, yellower and yellower. Pure, unadulterated fear had struck Owl. His eyes now resembled two golden full Moons, almost never blinking. They have remained like that ever since that fateful day. As if that wasn't enough, Wisakachak, holding Owl by the top of his head, picked up some mud and began to rub it all over the hapless bird.

"From this day on, you nosy bird, you will wear this drab mud color." Wisakachak continued rubbing dirt into Owl's feathers. "You will have the most unwanted job on the planet. You will be the Harbinger of Death. You will not rest as others do. You will remain awake all night, every night. Furthermore, you annoying bird," ranted Wisakachak, "you will get very little rest during the day. Now get out of here, before I really lose my temper, you feathered freak."

Ghost Woman
Blackfoot/Woodland Cree legend

Here's a scary *story for around the campfire.*

He pulled the bowstring back and, allowing for the wind, let the arrow fly. It was true to its mark, hitting Deer high in the chest and piercing a vital organ. The creature dropped to its knees with its eyes already glazed, tongue lolling from its mouth as it fell to the forest floor. The young Wood Cree rose from his crouched position and started forward to claim his prize. But just as he got to the fallen carcass of Deer, he was struck form behind by a powerful blow. His head seemed to explode and all went black as his knees buckled beneath him.

Some time later the scouts dragged the Wood Cree man before the Elders of the Blackfoot.

"We found him hunting in the forest near our encampment," said a Blackfoot scout, pushing the Wood Cree forward. The Elders looked at the young, captive Warrior who stood before them with his head held high. He showed no fear of the Blackfoot. There was blood still streaming from his head wound where the club had struck him. He smiled at his captors.

His bravery impressed the Elders so much they told the scouts to release him. His bonds were quickly cut with a sharp knife. It was obvious by the scars that covered a great deal of his body that, at some time or other, he had tangled with Bear. The Bear-claw necklace he wore told all Bear was not the winner in the confrontation.

"A brave man, indeed, that would fight mighty Bear," said one of the Elders.

"What are you doing in the Land of the Blackfoot?" asked another.

"I am just moving about, hunting, trying to stay alive," the Wood Cree answered arrogantly.

The Elders spoke softly among themselves and then told the Chief of their decision.

The Chief stood and said, "Let him go." He then waved the Blackfoot warriors away from the Wood Cree. "You are welcome to stay with us Wood Cree. We would be proud to have such a brave, young man among our People. Or, if you wish, you may leave when you are ready. We will not interfere again." The Chief smiled at the brave, young man.

The young man decided to stay and settled into the community quite well. Even though badly scarred, he was handsome and brave and a great and fearless hunter. He soon became a great favorite with the girls of the Tribe but he would lay with none of them. The young men and women started to wonder about this soft-spoken, handsome, young Wood Cree.

One night he was sitting among some other young Warriors and girls listening to the Story Keeper tell the story of Creation. After the account, the Story Keeper asked, "Wood Cree, we would very much like to hear a little about you?"

One of the young Warriors spoke out, saying, "Why do you not take a woman? There are many that would be yours for the asking."

The Wood Cree looked reluctant to speak and stared for a while at his feet. Then, looking up at the Story Keeper, he said, "It is time that all knew the strange thing that befell me." He sat back and got himself comfortable and then started his story.

"At the time when the buds become fat and the Frogs sing, I went to hunt for my family. It had been a long, hard Winter and we had very little food left. Many times during that Winter, we had gone hungry. So it was important that I get a Buffalo or at least a Deer to refill our parfleches. I headed towards the mountains. In the foothills, I found Deer and managed to kill one. I carried it back to my lodge and that night, as my daughter slept, my wife and I went outside and skinned the animal and dressed the hide by the light of our fire. My wife made a pot of soup with some of the meat, and I went to the Lodge to wake our little one so she could have something good to eat. She was not there. Of course, my wife and I became very alarmed and we searched the lodge thoroughly. She was not to be found. We then set out to search the surrounding area. There was no Moon and it was very dark. We called to our little one but there was no answer, our search was fruitless.

"Exhausted, we returned to the lodge and vowed to renew the search at first light. We lay down in the lodge and I tried to comfort my distraught wife as she sobbed. Suddenly, we heard our child crying. Her cries seemed to come from beneath where we lay. We quickly got up and pulled back the sleeping robes but found nothing. Again our child's muffled wail appeared to come from under the sod. My wife and I took digging sticks and frantically started to dig the earth from the lodge floor, all the time listening to our child moaning and weeping. As we dug, bones began to appear. We dug with more haste, not understanding the meaning of this strange find. We found more bones which seemed to be those of a woman. The moans of our child, mysteriously changed to the voice of a woman. Suddenly, our child was back, laying on a Buffalo robe close to us. My wife grabbed the baby and headed to the opening of the lodge."

"Let us leave here immediately, husband. There is evil in this place," she said in a very frightened voice. "Before she could reach the exit, the woman's voice demanded, 'Give me the child.' The voice seemed to come from the bones that still lay in a heap on the lodge floor."

"Go away," screamed my terrified wife. "What is happening here? Do something," she demanded of me.

"Who are you?" I demanded.

"I am the ghost of the woman whose bones you unceremoniously displaced," said the weird ghost voice.

"We are sorry if we disturbed you," I said nervously, then I asked. "Why do you want our child?"

"I was the wife of a famous war Chief but, during my life, I was barren and bore him no children. Even so, he was good to me. I missed being a mother. Now, I will take your baby. I will enjoy motherhood as most other women have. I will reward you, young man, if you give me the child. It is only a girl, after all. You will have many more children. You can spare this one," said the ghost.

"My husband, let us leave this place, now," begged my wife.

"It is very dark outside. We must wait until the light comes," was my answer.

We settled down and all seemed well for a while, my wife clinging to our child and peering apprehensively around the lodge.

"Young man, I will make you a great hunter and brave warrior. I will give you special powers over others. Please give me the child," pleaded the voice.

"I did not answer, but I was starting to wonder if this Ghost Woman actually could give me these powers."

"Young man, I will be a second wife to you," she continued. "I will come to you in the night. You will never see me, but you may have me in any way you wish. I will be your slave. I will make beautiful clothes for you. I will make Magic for you." Then, she demanded again, "Give me the child."

"No," shouted my wife. She looked at me and pleaded, 'Please don't do this, My husband, tears welling up in her big, brown eyes. I ignored her. I was now under the spell of the Ghost Woman.

"You will have more children, my wife. Give me the child. I fear if we do not give her to the Ghost Woman, we will never leave this place." My wife refused to give up our child, so I tore the little one from her arms and held her out in front of me, as my wife ran from the lodge. I saw nothing but the child was taken from me. With a heavy heart but also hoping that what the Ghost had promised would transpire, I went to bed.

"Much later that night, as I lay sleeping, what I thought was my wife returned and crawled into our sleeping robes, her warm, naked body snuggled down beside me. Soon, we were making passionate love, the like of which I had never experienced with her before. It was a night I will never forget. Eventually, exhausted, I drifted off into a deep sleep. When I woke up in the morning, the Sunlight was shining into my lodge through the smoke hole. I looked around for my erotic mate. All that lay beside me were the bones of the Ghost Woman. They had been my partner the night before. I may never take a real woman again.

"The Ghost Woman still visits me but only on occasions. It is my punishment for giving up my little girl, my own flesh and blood. I have never seen my wife since." The young Wood Cree Warrior finished his eerie story and all around the camp fire were hushed. As he stood to leave the Fire Circle some say that they plainly heard a woman's voice call the young man back to his lodge.

The next morning, the encampment was bursting with news of the Wood Cree story. Some Elders went to his lodge to talk to him further about his strange tale. As they entered his lodge, a cold, chilling wind seemed to come from inside. The Wood Cree was nowhere to be found. He was never seen again.

Letting Go
Plains Cree/Blood legend

Here's a story of love and death.

Just before the White Men came to the Plains, there lived a young, beautiful couple. Their love for each other was such that they had become man and wife. In fact, it is said never had two People been so much in love. Just to be near these lovers would gladden your heart. They were a delight. They always dressed in the finest clothes which the young wife made for them both with painstaking devotion. The woman's hair was always at its best. It shone like the Raven's wing and her smile would melt the sternest heart. The young husband kept himself clean and immaculately dressed. His hair was perfectly braided, and he consistently had good words for everyone. As you can well imagine, these lovers were great favorites with everyone in the village. Their happiness was contagious.

One morning the young man woke up and looked over at his beautiful wife, who was still peacefully sleeping. "I will make her breakfast as a surprise," he thought. He went outside and cheerfully set about his chores. He started a fire and cooked them both a fine breakfast. He took two steaming bowls of food into their lodge and placed them near his sleeping wife. He then attempted to shake her out of her deep sleep. She didn't move. He shook her a little harder. She still didn't move. The unthinkable entered his head, as he shook her again, this time quite violently. The terrible reality dawned. His loving young wife had passed into the Spirit World during the night.

The young man ran from his lodge, screaming and crying. The warriors immediately came to arms, thinking the village was under attack but the women knew better. On seeing the grieving husband, they realized what must have happened. Some went into his lodge to look after his wife's remains while others led the distraught young man away, trying their best to comfort him in his time of uncontrollable grief.

After his wife's untimely death, the young man fell apart. His nature totally changed. He became rude and intolerant of others. He neither bathed nor took care of any of his personal requirements. For a while his behavior was permitted and the Elders tried to counsel him, to bring his grieving to an end, but he would not listen to them. Of course, there was the normal mourning period respectfully called for by the Elders. But soon it came time for the living to get on with their lives.

When that time came, the Elders went to the young man and told him that his behavior would no longer be tolerated. The young man packed up his belongings and left the village. He headed into the mountains where he set up his lodge in the wilderness, and would sit for many hours thinking and brooding about his wife, mourning her loss, consumed with sadness.

The young man who had always been such a fastidious person in everything to do with his appearance now let himself go completely. His hair hung in dirty, uncombed tresses and was now left unbraided. His face and body were filthy. His clothes tattered and torn. He had become a pathetic shadow of his former self. The man had stopped caring for even his most basic needs.

One morning he was sitting, still feeling sorry for himself, when off in the distance he saw a pony and rider approaching his camp. "Good," he thought, "maybe it is an enemy, and when he finds me, he will kill me. Then perhaps I will be able to be with my beautiful wife again."

As the pony and rider got closer, he was sure he recognized his dead wife as the rider. But it could not be. This woman, although she resembled his wife, was slovenly and filthy. "My wife would not let herself get into such a mess," he thought. The pony and rider were almost at his camp, when in recognition he shouted, "It is you, my wife, you have returned from the dead." Even with his rejoicing, he was confused. He asked, "Why are you this way? What has happened to your beautiful clothes? Why is your hair not combed? It is so dirty. I have never seen you this way. Have you come from the Spirit World? If so, why are you filthy? I thought that World, would be a wonderful, clean place."

"Oh, it is, my husband, but I cannot go there. You see, I have become the mirror of you. Take a good look at yourself. You are as filthy as I am. You are the reason I am this way because you will not let me go to Creator. Until you stop grieving and let the sadness go from your heart, I cannot enter the Spirit World. Please, don't be frightened to let the power of Creator help you heal. There will be a magic in letting go of your grief. My husband, mourning too long has become an obstacle to your need."

"It is you that I need. How can I let you go, I loved you much more than life itself," sobbed the husband.

"No, what you need, my beloved husband, is happiness. You must let go of your sadness. Just remember our good times, only the times that bring smiles to your lips. Good memories can keep our love alive. You must let your heartache and anger go or it will destroy you."

The man closed his eyes, thinking over his wife's words. When he looked up, his wife was gone, but he now understood he had to let the painful recollections of his wife's passing go. He tore off his dirty clothes and bathed in a nearby stream, thinking of all the good times he had been given with his beautiful wife. He cried unashamedly but these were tears of happiness that streamed down his face. And these happy thoughts were reflections of all the joy she had brought him.

Letting go had finally allowed his loved one to enter the beautiful, Red World of the Spirits where she now belonged and him, the right to continue a normal life.

Some other *Gift/Souvenir* titles from PREMIUM PRESS AMERICA include:

America The Beautiful

Baby, A Bundle of Joy

I'll Be Doggone

Cats Out of the Bag

Bill Dance Fishing Tips

Civil War Trivia

Golf Trivia

Titanic Trivia

Dream Catchers

Story Keepers

Great American Guide to Fine Wines

Great American Outdoors

Great American Women

I Love You, Mom

Moms Are Very Special

Angels Everywhere

Snow Angels

Miracles: Inspiring Stories of Hope

Power of Prayer

Absolutely Alabama

Amazing Arkansas

Fabulous Florida

Gorgeous Georgia

Legendary Louisiana (coming soon)

Mighty Mississippi

Naturally North Carolina (coming soon)

Sensational South Carolina

Terrific Tennessee

Tremendous Texas

Vintage Virginia

For more information contact:

PREMIUM PRESS AMERICA
P.O. Box 159015
Nashville, Tennessee 37211
800.891.7323
615.256.8484 *voice*
615.256.8624 *fax*

PREMIUM PRESS AMERICA *Gift/Souvenir* books are distributed nationwide. If, by chance, none are available in your local area books can be ordered direct from The Publisher. For more information contact premiumpressamerica.com